THE SYSTEM

T0346483

THE SYSTEM

STAN KOLODZIEJ

THAMES RIVER PRESS

The System

THAMES RIVER PRESS
An imprint of Wimbledon Publishing Company Limited (WPC)
Another imprint of WPC is Anthem Press (www.anthempress.com)
First published in the United Kingdom in 2014 by
THAMES RIVER PRESS
75–76 Blackfriars Road
London SE1 8HA

www.thamesriverpress.com

All the characters and events described in this novel are imaginary
and any similarity with real people or events is purely coincidental.

A CIP record for this book is available from the British Library.

ISBN 978-1-78308-132-5

This title is also available as an eBook

To those sleepwalkers about to awaken

Prologue

They saw unmarked cars parked on the street outside the hotel. This time they were watching me, waiting. It was like a performance. And the audience was getting restless. The actress hadn't come out yet. Maybe she never would.

Morning came. Friday. I hoped I had enough nerve to go through with it. Fear was waiting for me again. It was always there now. At 1:30 p.m. I was outside the station. I didn't hide. I was through with that. They had to be on time. I didn't know how much longer I could wait.

Finally I saw the three of them leave through the back of the station. I walked over to one of the trash bins and took out the paper bag with Kaz's plywood and bomb. I waited right there with the package. No one stopped me, no one even noticed.

There's that stop sign before you turn onto 35th coming out of the station. That's where I waited. In a few minutes the car appeared. There was a lot of traffic on 8th. They could be waiting there for some time. I left the package on the street and walked away. The car pulled up and stopped, right over the package. I could see Copernik in the driver's seat. Vecchio was not in the car. That prick had nine lives. No man in the suit either. Just Copernik. That was OK. That would do for now.

Two police cars pulled into the station parking lot. One of the officers looked at me closely as they passed by. I could see he was trying to add it together, trying to get the letters to click and tumble, trying to come up with an answer.

Another police car pulled out of the station parking lot and started coming towards the exit, right behind Copernik's car. There was more traffic than I ever saw those days watching the station, it was like a regular freeway.

I turned for a moment and knew Copernik saw me. I don't know what he could have been thinking. He must have wondered what I was doing there. Maybe at that second he knew what was coming. Maybe we resign ourselves to things faster than we think. We don't even know it. It's just a matter of catching up to it.

I tried to detonate the package with the cellphone but nothing happened. Maybe Kaz was fucking with me one last time. Copernik hit the accelerator and the bomb went off and the back of the car disintegrated. That was that. I just kept walking towards the car. Go straight at the lion, right? I wouldn't have more than a few seconds. The two officers in the car behind were already getting out. Copernik was still moving in there. It was weird. There were no flames. It was more like a concussion bomb. Kaz must have done something wrong when he made it. Figures. The back of the car was lifted up and came back down a few feet like it had been punched from beneath and then from above. The two back tires burst and the back windshield shattered. That was all.

I walked up, didn't run or slow down or crouch like in the fucking manual, and while I was walking I pumped a lot of rounds into what was left of the car. I could see Copernik still reaching for his gun. I ejected the empty magazine from the Glock and fumbled with a new one. It was a matter of seconds, either way. I relaxed just enough for it to make a difference. Yeah, I made the mistake, after all that training, of lowering my gun while I reloaded. Copernik raised his gun just as I got my new clip in, aimed and fired. It was all over in a few seconds.

That other training, the Mozambique Drill and going for the cranial cavity and the obdulla longella, or whatever it's fucking called, it's all bullshit. I didn't aim, just kept firing, until all the bullets were gone, until whatever I was aiming at didn't move anymore. Copernik was just a big shadow to me; he could have been anyone, anything, in there. I just wanted him to be still.

When I stopped there was no more moving inside the car. Copernik had sagged against the driver side door, very still, and his eyes had that faraway look. I started walking away. Police were coming out of the building and cars now. Some cars were stopping on the street, people getting out. I remembered now that something shot past me when the bomb went off, part of the car maybe, then something hit me in the shoulder. I looked back. I saw the little guy in the suit. He was looking at me. He raised his gun and fired. Something smacked into the wall a few feet behind me. Then I heard someone shouting to stop firing. I thought at first they were yelling at me. I couldn't remember firing any more shots.

I staggered then ran and didn't look back. I walked in the opposite direction of the warehouse on 8th. After a while I stopped and then began to walk again. It's nothing, I told myself, and kept walking. I could hear police cars behind me. There was no time. They would be here any second. A change of plan. I tossed the cellphone into a trash bin. When I reached the office building on 32nd I entered the lobby. Someone shouted at me. It was the man in the suit. He was right there this time, in the blind spot with me. Everyone in the lobby scattered. He raised his gun again and I ignored him. He looked pissed off, like I had betrayed him. He could do what he wanted. I went through the door to the stairs going to the parking levels. No one shouted at me, no one fired. Something told me they wouldn't.

I reached the third level of the parking garage, just as Kaz had mapped it for me.

In a few moments I was through the maintenance door and the little rabbit was in the maze again. The police had missed blocking this one. I was in the tunnels one more time. I had to keep going, I couldn't black out. It was so quiet. There were no police, no one was behind me. They had seen me go into the parking garage. They would find the door, they must have already found it.

I heard people talking ahead in the tunnels. They had to be the police. I went to the surface and into the city again, coming out on 27th Street through an office building. I began walking towards Penn Station. I could see a police car turn onto 27th heading my way. I went through the nearest door and into a small clothing store. The young woman behind the counter looked up and smiled at me, and then her face got real serious.

I had to sit. I was starting to black out, but there were no chairs so I leaned against the wall and closed my eyes. If I didn't close my eyes I knew I would collapse. The only shopper in the store, a middle-aged woman, looked at me when I first came in. You could hear the police sirens in the distance, a few streets away. When I opened my eyes again, I saw her looking directly at me. You could see her putting it together. It was only a few seconds before she would be getting her cellphone out. I wasn't sure what I was going to do. It was like I was watching myself, like the others, not having a clue what would happen.

The young woman left the counter and surprised me by coming over and putting her hand on my shoulder. She spoke to me like she knew me, like she was expecting me. I didn't say anything. It was the last thing I expected. She led me towards the counter. Her hand was on my back and I could feel the blood there getting cold against my skin. The young woman said something to the shopper. I don't know what she said but the middle-aged woman said something back then left the store.

The young woman led me into the back of the store. There were cloth cutting tools and opened boxes filled with clothes everywhere. She got an old armchair from the corner, pulled it out and sat me in it.

She started to take my coat off and I panicked. Who was she? Did the whole city know about me? I pulled out my gun and pointed it at her and she backed away and stared at me.

She asked me if I had been shot. I said I thought I had been. I didn't know. Maybe it was the bomb or part of the car. Was any of it real? I couldn't be sure.

She knew about me. By some city jungle tom-toms she knew about the bombing at the radical center. She said she could try and get me out of the city, that she knew people. Everybody knew people. I had enough of it.

I told her that I didn't need help. I just needed to get to the street again. I started to get up again then collapsed. I was so tired. She made a call on her cellphone and then said there were police everywhere. We would wait. I had to let the world turn in this woman's hands.

After a while she started to take my coat off again. This time I let her.

She retrieved some bandages from another room, then took my shirt off and looked at my back and I heard her gasp. So that was it. I was dying. She stared at the wound for some time before she got a small towel from a restroom and started to get some of the blood off. She put bandages on the wound and taped them in place. We heard the door to the shop open again. She looked at me. She turned completely white. Then she went into the shop again. I heard her talking to another woman, then I heard the door close and the click of it being locked.

When she returned she had a new blouse in her hands. She put it on me. It wasn't easy. I could only lift my arm a few inches and even that was painful. When she was finished she sat across from me and smiled. She was terrified. I could see that she now regretted her rash decision. I had walked into her life and now she was in too deep. Her little game of revolution had gone too far, it was too real. I was just another embarrassment. I could see her mind working out how to get rid of me now.

I had to hand it to her. She didn't try and talk about it. She didn't ask why, didn't try and see how it all fit the pattern of her worldview, how I could try and make her understand how all the pieces fit together. I don't think I could have done it anyway. Suddenly it was all about survival. That was all that mattered.

I didn't ask how she knew, how any of them knew. I didn't care.

A door opened somewhere at the back of the store and the young woman bolted up and rushed into one of the back rooms. A young man with a beard poked his head in and looked at me, then he was gone and I heard them talking. There was talk of the reward and the young woman was angry, telling him that he had to be quiet, that I was dying, that I needed help. That I was armed, maybe dangerous. Let them argue. I got up and went back through the shop to the front door. I had to get out of there. Tired of the sitting, the waiting. I had never been good at that. There was no activity on the street. No police cars. Everyone was on alert, looking around, wondering what was happening. Waiting for the big one, always waiting for the big one in this paranoid what-the-fuck-are-you-looking-at country of mine. There was a quiet in the storm; they were waiting for it to begin again. Fuck 'em. They would know what it was about soon enough.

I unlocked the door and went out again. Putting one foot in front of the other, moving ahead, looking at no one. Let my feet do the walking. Taking me somewhere, as long as I was moving, just keep moving. I could see the roof of Penn Station now. It looked a hundred miles away. I looked at the subway entrance nearby but I was done with the tunnels. They could shoot me instead this time. I didn't think I could make it out anyway. I would die there, in that darkness. No, I couldn't do it.

I rested several times, leaning against walls, trying not to let my legs fold under me, because I knew that once I went down, there was no getting up again. A car pulled up beside me and I saw it was a cab. The young woman from the shop was in the passenger seat, motioning for me to get into the cab. The driver was the man who had peeked in to look at me.

A police car was coming along the street. The driver saw it and panicked. The young woman left the cab and asked me to get in. She was begging. The driver was now screaming at her to get back into the car.

The young woman said that I must trust her. She had made her decision, despite the fear that consumed her, she had made her decision and risked all to help me. And she had dragged her boyfriend along with her. It seemed that everything she believed in hinged on this one act of mine. It was all so familiar.

I let her lead me into the cab. The police car picked up speed then went by. The young man pulled us away from the curb and we followed the traffic.

Then she gave me an earful of bullshit. She said that she admired me, what I was doing, that she would never have the nerve to do it herself. She looked at me like a star-struck teenager, a worshiper in front of an idol. She sounded like she was talking about someone in the past. Like I was as good as dead. Maybe she was right. Maybe I was and just hadn't caught up to it yet. I wasn't even paying attention to her. She was talking some crap about the Occupy Wall Street movement, how everyone just wanted to be part of a movement, any movement, like they belonged, like they were making a difference. It was all I could do not to shoot her. All the time I was watching the young man, who kept glancing in the rear-view mirror at us. I could tell he had already made up his mind. The tumblers had really clicked for this guy. He was going after the reward, the glory. Maybe this stupid girl didn't even know that yet, or maybe she was just keeping me busy on the way to the police.

I asked the driver where we were going. He said nowhere, we were just driving around. But I knew they were just waiting for me to die. Then they would pull into a police station and that would be it. I had to smile. I knew it would be the Midtown South Station, only a few blocks away. When you're dying, they say, the sense of irony becomes acute. Maybe they know what they are talking about.

"Where do you want us to go?" he asked.

I didn't answer. We were heading towards Penn Station. I didn't know if it was by chance or if they had guessed it. Did I tell them before? No, I didn't think so. but I couldn't be sure.

The young woman had tears in her eyes now. Why was she crying? Because of guilt? Because I was dying?

"We have to get you to a hospital," the young woman said. The young man glanced back again. There was anger in his eyes.

I told them no hospital.

"How much is the reward?" I asked the young man.

He didn't answer. The young woman said it was half a million.

"You killed some people," the young man said. "You deserve what you get."

The young woman told him to be quiet. I told him he knew shit about any of this.

"When you passed out we were going to take your gun," she said, "then drive to a police station. I'm sorry."

I told the driver to pull the car over. We were heading away from the train station.

He kept driving.

"There's a police car ahead," he said. "I'll let you off at the next block."

When he pulled over I got out. I had to lean against the door to prevent passing out.

The young woman was crying again.

"Please let us take you to a hospital," she pleaded.

The young man said that I wouldn't make it. The first bit of truth I heard from him. I told him to keep driving.

The young woman reached out and handed me something. It was a bottle of aspirin and a bottle of water. She wished me good luck and said she was sorry. The young man left the car and came around to face me. I pulled out my gun and pointed it at him. I knew I would have killed him on the spot. I wouldn't have hesitated. It surprised me how easily I would have done it.

His face was full of hate. I didn't know him and yet he hated me so much. He shouted at the young woman that she should have taken the gun from me a long time ago. I asked her if she wanted to leave the car, leave him, but she shook her head. I told the prick to get back in the car. He hesitated and looked around. There were a few pedestrians, not many. There were no police. I knew what he was thinking. I told him that I would shoot him right there if he thought of drawing any attention to us. He gauged how serious I was.

"You're fucking done anyway," he said, then got back into the cab.

"Can I come with you?" the girl asked me. I didn't answer her. It was so ludicrous. There was nowhere to go.

She finally got in the car and they drove off.

I had to get off the street. They might be back again. They might lead the police to me. They could still claim the reward. My head was starting to spin.

There was only one thing to do. I entered the fucking tunnels again. This time everything was quiet down there. No police, no maintenance workers, no mole people, only the distant sounds of subway trains. Everything had gone up to the surface. There was nothing left down here except quiet.

I took some of the aspirin and began to walk. These tunnels were a part of me now; I could find my way around them more easily than on the streets. I found the city now made me dizzy. The light at the surface confused me. What was happening? Was I changing into something else, a new creature, a new life form?

I saw something move ahead, then I heard voices. I stood there, unable to move or hide. Three people came out of one of the tunnels. They saw me and stopped. They were three teenagers, urban explorers. I looked at their outfits, the knee-high boots and headlamps and the ropes and GPS systems and I started laughing. It wasn't that long ago that I wore the same gear in these tunnels.

They stared at me like I was a ghost. One of them, a young girl, came forward to get a closer look.

"You're the one," she said. "It's all over the internet. Why are you still in the city?"

I collapsed.

They came over and helped me get to my feet again. I kept walking. I had to move, keep going.

"We're for you," one of them said. "We believe in what you're doing."

It sounded so hollow, so insincere.

I kept walking and they didn't follow or try and stop me. There would be more like them in the tunnels soon. With their gear and their need to join something, to become part of something, anything, any movement. They were everywhere. This was something they could tell their friends, something they could brag about when they were getting laid. Maybe there would even be tours in the future; it would become a tourist curiosity, like those underground bunkers from the wars. Maybe they were planning on keeping me here, like a cool revolutionary pet. A species nearly extinct.

What I wouldn't give to be back exploring again, freaked out by every shadow and sound down here.

Then I blacked out. When I came to I was in one of our storage rooms, lying on a mattress. The three urban explorers were kneeling in front of me. I asked them what time it was. I had been out for half an hour. I tried to get up but there was too much pain.

"We have to get you out of here," the girl said. "I tried to fix it a little but you've lost a lot of blood."

She was nice enough for a sleepwalker. They're always nice. They have so little else to give. I wanted to go back to sleepwalking, exploring these tunnels.

I thanked her and tried to get up again. It was then that I noticed my gun was no longer in my coat pocket.

"You looked a little strange to us, so we took it, just in case," one of them said, apologizing.

I asked them where they were from.

"NYU," they said. They looked so young. I felt so old.

The boy offered the gun back to me. I told him to keep it. He stared at it with reverence. Maybe he would build a shrine around it one day. Part of the tour.

Then the boy asked if the police would need it for their investigation. One of the others told him to shut up.

"But you shot somebody with this," the boy said. "Didn't you?"

I told him the prick deserved it. And more. I told him again to keep it or get rid of it. It didn't matter to me. I was done with it. He gave it back to me and I put the gun in my bag.

They helped me to my feet and I started walking again.

"You're walking in the wrong direction," the girl said, "if you're going to the station."

She was right. I was walking away from the station. Big revolutionary can't even walk in the right direction. They helped me the rest of the way. I asked them why they didn't turn me in. They only shrugged. They couldn't answer that. I must have looked that pathetic to them. We walked in silence. There was nothing more to say and I was thankful they didn't ask any questions. What kind of philosophy brought her to this place? I wouldn't know where to begin. I appreciated their respect. Especially their silence.

When we got to the station I thanked them and told them to leave before the authorities found us. I sounded like a mother scolding her children. Before they left the girl kissed my cheek and squeezed my hand and wished me good luck. I brushed away her tears. I was tired of tears, pain and suffering. It was all I seemed good for now – causing pain and suffering. I needed to hear laughter, to feel joy, to make someone's pain go away. I didn't know how to do that.

I watched until they were gone and then I went through the access tunnel into Pennsylvania Plaza.

I entered the main concourse at the station and went into one of the restroom stalls and took out the iodine and bandages and tried to stop the bleeding in my shoulder as best as I could. It was hard to reach the back of my shoulder. The pain almost made me pass out. It was all I could do for now.

I glanced at the stalls, thinking that maybe Kaz was on the other side of one of them, waiting for the credit card to appear. Maybe Jimmy would be waiting for me out there in the station. I was losing focus, losing the sense of where I was. I picked up my bag and got on the train. I had to leave the city. I felt that if I didn't, the tunnels would swallow me for good. I needed to feel the daylight, even if it meant no escape. I didn't care. I needed to be moving away from the city. Anywhere.

A woman entered the restroom and one of the stalls. There was something familiar about her. I wasn't sure. Had I seen her somewhere else? Where? No, it's common. Fear changes faces, the mind projects and you have little control over it. She left the stall and came over to wash her hands. I froze and waited. I could barely breathe. The woman finished and left without a word, without glancing at me. I felt relieved. Maybe I didn't draw any attention. I stayed there a long time and looked at myself in the mirror. I had been pretty, once. Now I was emaciated, thin and pale. I took off my baseball cap. My hair was thinner, darker. I was morphing into one of the creatures in the tunnels. Even the pupils in my eyes were disappearing. I needed sun and fresh air. That's all. Getting better was just a matter of time.

I took what was left of the aspirins and left.

I bought some awful coffee from a machine and sat in the waiting area, with my back to the glass. As far away from anyone as possible. I kept myself awake. If I slept now I would be lost. My eyes were glued to the departures board, watching the white numbers and letters clatter, disappear and reform, time and again. I was waiting for the right answer.

I thought of going back to my friend the intern again, but I knew it would be the end of him. He had risked enough for me. I didn't think I could make it anyway.

Fuck it. We made our choices. I made mine. I was living them right now.

There were no police around the station. What could that mean? Did they forget about me? No, impossible. It was so quiet there in that corner, a little refuge. Maybe I was invisible.

I felt someone's hand on my shoulder and I startled. I was asleep. It was an old woman. Her face was so kind. Was she an angel? She asked me if I was alright. I thanked her and told her that yes, I was OK, just tired. There was a little blood on my chair but I didn't think she noticed it. I thanked her again and she moved away and was gone in the crowd.

The letters and numbers were tumbling again. What mysterious answer will they come up with? And then I saw it. My train was ready.

I used the ticket I bought a few days before and boarded the Lake Shore Limited to Chicago. As soon as I leave the train I'll get someone to look at my shoulder, I thought. I just need to get away first. It was simple. I was feeling better.

I'm on the train now writing all this. I can't tell you where I'm going. I don't really know myself.

Maybe I'll go to a South American country and join a revolution. Maybe I'll just disappear, maybe in Chicago, never go into a subway again. Find that final big blind spot. For good. Yeah sure.

They'll have to catch me. I'm not going to walk up to them. Let them get me. I'm not going to make it easy for them.

They can try and find me if they want.

That's up to The System. I don't care now.

I just need to rest. Just rest a little. The pain in my shoulder is better, but I'm tired. The train is slowing down. They've announced we're getting close to the next station. Maybe I'll get off here. I don't know.

I need to write it all down. I'll start to write right now. No, when I'm feeling better, later, I'll find a quiet place, somewhere quiet, and just write. Alone, no more dark places, out in the air and the sun, somewhere where it's quiet. I can get better there and write. It was so simple.

There's a little girl sitting across from me with her mother. The little girl's smiling at me. I'm crying. I don't know why. Maybe because she reminds me of that young girl in the tunnels. I never learned her name. The one I buried yesterday, close to Jimmy and Kaz. All that time down there and I never learned her name, never asked her what her name was. It somehow didn't seem right, having names in those tunnels. Names were for the surface, the city, The System. The tunnels were a place to be reborn, with no names.

I don't want to upset the girl sitting in front of me. I'm trying to smile, but I can only cry now. I think of that little girl in the tunnels and I'm ashamed. I let her down. I was responsible for her. I should have brought her to the city. The girl asks her mother why I'm crying. They believe adults know everything. The mother looks at me, not knowing what to make of me, and tells the little girl that she is not sure. I smile but there is no sympathy in the woman's eyes, only the little girl seems to care about me. There is no one else I can turn to. I hope the mother lets her stay there, close to me. Her compassion means everything in the world to me now. It's all I have left.

I drop my pen and the girl climbs down and picks it up for me. She can see how much pain I'm in. I'm angry at myself for letting her see it.

The girl asks me if I'm hurt. I tell her no, and it makes me cry even more. Such innocence, God, such beautiful innocence. I don't know what else to say. Then, to my surprise, the girl begins to hum and brushes my hair. The mother moves forwards to stop her but I tell her it's alright. I must look like fright night by now. I tell the girl that I'm feeling better and thank her.

I just need to close my eyes. The brushing feels good. I don't regret what we've done. We all use The System, maybe sometimes as much as it uses us. Jimmy, Kaz and I, we're no better.

I only wish we had done more. I wish we were just starting now. I hate it all more now than when we started. When I get through this I'm going to start again. I'm going to fuck The System as much as I can. Maybe there's another way to do it. A better way. I don't know.

No, there isn't. I know there isn't. We can only try and take it down one piece at a time. Even if I have to try it alone. Jimmy was right.

I just need to rest. I try not to think about what happened during those past few weeks.

It's no use.

1
THE PACT

Early on, we made a pact not to get trapped by any ideology. We didn't believe in any of them. Anarchy, nihilism, socialism, fucking social Darwinists, you name it. All bullshit. Somebody always wants to lead and they always want others to follow. That's the way it is.

With the three of us, it became a suicide pact. We knew we wouldn't survive, not with what we were going to do. It was simple revenge. At least, that's how it started. That's how we looked at it.

I think it really started in high school, that summer night we burned every book we had about anarchy and philosophy. We actually burned them in a childish ceremony in the back yard of Jimmy's house. We ran when a neighbor called the police and the firemen came. We laughed all the way down the street. Jimmy was told he couldn't see me for a few weeks. He couldn't even leave the house for a week. It was all great. I think that was when it started, on that night of purification.

My mom called Jimmy's mom and there was shit to pay. That was right at the end of the summer. By the time Jimmy and I saw each other again we were going off to college. I think our parents had planned it that way, although my mom laughed and told me I was crazy. But I knew they were trying to keep us apart. Maybe they knew something we didn't know about each other. Like some animals can smell fear or trouble. Looking back, I think I would have done the same thing if I'd been one of the parents. No question.

Jimmy and I talked on the phone for a while and then wrote letters/emails, and then you know what happens. We just lost touch and went our separate ways.

I didn't see Jimmy again for four years, until after college. I loved him, I think I had known it even before then, and I became jealous of that friend of his with the weird name. Because I knew Jimmy didn't love me; and if he had loved me he would come home from school, looking for me. Wanting to be with me.

How long ago was that? Just a few years? Really, we were just kids. I don't think that, at that point, any of us knew what would happen next. No, it was impossible to know. I still don't understand how it happened.

I think it was that night with the books. We were frustrated at what had happened to our families, at what we were seeing around us. As we got older we could see more, everything became clearer, like those slides that you put over other slides until everything starts to come into focus and you see a world that you never knew was there.

That's when we first started to see The System.

It was all around us. It was incredible. It was like that movie where everything is normal until you put on these special glasses and you see the aliens all around. And you realize just how much you're a part of it and how much it is a part of you. That's why you can't see it.

That's why we burned those books. They were all about their own systems. They all wanted to make you a part of their system. In a way they were just as bad as any of those companies trying to sell you something. At least with those companies you can see the furniture and the cars they're hawking. You know what they're trying to do. There's no hiding it. They want to fuck you and make you feel good about it.

I went over to Jimmy's mother's place a few times when I was home from college, and she said he hardly ever came home anymore, especially after the first year. He had a friend with a funny name, from school, and they went off together, did odd jobs, hitchhiked and did other crazy things. She didn't like this friend he was hanging out with. That's the thing with mothers, right? There's always somebody they think is fucking up their kid's life. I didn't know at the time that one of those somebodies would be me.

The friend lived somewhere in Queens. Jimmy's mom said he was a troublemaker. She was in rough shape at that point. Her husband had died the year before. She didn't mind Jimmy being away, because he had enough money to get through school. She was worried how Jimmy was getting the money, and what he and his friend were up to. She was afraid of what would happen to her son. Soon both of us were worried about it.

I could tell Jimmy's mom knew I was in love with him. I could see in her eyes that she wanted me to go find him and see what he was up to, and talk to him. She wanted me to bring him home. She knew I did too.

Jimmy's mom only had a name, Kaz, and knew that he lived in Queens. I was furious with Jimmy, with what he was doing to his mother, and I told her that I would find him and bring him home. I never brought him back.

It took me a few days and some digging at Queens College to find the address. It was in Flushing. Not a nice neighborhood. I was there in a few hours. While I was waiting, someone in the apartment building said Jimmy and his friend worked in the city and took the number seven subway train back to Main Street in Queens. I was nervous talking with these people. They were tough and they had those eyes - the kind of eyes always probing to get something from you, find a weak spot and then move in.

I waited at the subway station for several hours, watching the people go down and come out of the tunnels. They seemed so strange to me, like they were creatures coming out of an underground city. And then I saw them. I knew it was a stupid thing to do, waiting for them there. I panicked and was trying to get away when Jimmy saw me and called my name. I should've kept going. I shouldn't have turned back. He looked puzzled. I told him that I had talked to his mother and that she was worried. Jimmy only smiled at me. "Were you worried, Ann?" he asked me.

I was embarrassed and said I wasn't worried. I hated him, condescending prick, but he knew it was a lie. All this time I had been stealing glances at his friend, who was staring at me, and I didn't like what I saw. He was small and thin as a razor, with a huge jaw, and he had this half-smile you get sometimes in people, like they have this dirty little secret they might or might not share with you. And he just kept staring at me. He was just like the others, staring and waiting, only he wasn't tough. I just stared back a few times. Finally, he turned away. I'm not that shy.

And then I remembered him. Last year in high school, transfer student. Science type. Real loner, worse than us. Kaz. I remembered him now. Nobody had paid attention to this kid back then, and now he was here with Jimmy, his new best friend. We hated each other from the start. In those situations it never really gets better.

We went to some coffee shop and then talked all night. Something weird was happening. I hate to say it, I forgot about Jimmy's mom. At least I made him phone her later. Now that I think of it, that was one of the last times he ever spoke with her. Truth is, I didn't like Jimmy's mom, and I don't think he was that keen on her either. She had those same eyes, the probing, find-a-weakness kind, always trying to find an edge. I don't think she missed Jimmy all that much as long as he kept sending her money.

Like I said, something strange was going on that night. Everything outside that coffee shop became more and more meaningless. Even thinking about my family was weird, and they started to fade away. There was a new world forming around us: something that had always been inside us, was now coming out and locking us in. If you ever get that sense of clearness and purpose, if you ever experience it, maybe you know what I'm talking about. It's a scary and warm feeling, all at once. It reshapes you, right there. You feel you can do anything. It's why you're here, now you know why, now you know what to do.

I thought about the older people I'd seen, the ones walking around having no clue why they're here anymore, what it was all fucking about, something tugging at them deep inside. They don't know why or what it is, just a little tug that keeps nagging at them, reminding them that it had always been there, but had become harder to listen to.

Like I said, we lost touch with each other in college. I had no idea what Jimmy was up to, maybe taking accounting courses by then, or trying to get into business school. Who knows. Four years is a long time. And then something incredible happened.

I don't remember exactly how it happened, but our thoughts and our conversation became more serious. It was like something was guiding us to one specific thing. We just knew that it was the direction we needed to go in.

How about this for weird. Earlier that summer, after all three of us graduated, we moved back to our town. None of us knew the others were there. There was a coffee shop in town where we used to hang out in high school. That's where we almost saw each other again. We just happened to be there on the same day. And we never saw each other but there was some strange karma going on. I don't think it was an accident, us getting together. It was just like going back to those high school days, when we burned those books. Some weird shit was trying to bring us back together. I have to believe that.

Jimmy and I were nervous at first. Something had changed. We were the same, but deep down we were different. When we talked those first few days it was like we were feeling each other out, like we had secrets and we weren't sure we could trust the other if we told them. I think we were both afraid of what was happening to us.

We didn't have to be. It was soon pretty clear that all three of us had the same secrets, that we felt the same way about everything around us, about The System. It was inside us, had nothing to do with books or our heads. It had always been there. Inside us. That's the strongest kind of belief.

It wasn't long before we were talking about strange stuff, about doing. And we weren't embarrassed about it. We became more relaxed with each other. Even Kaz was warming up to me. Truth is, if Jimmy liked someone, then Kaz was OK with it, you get a pass, even though deep inside he hated your guts.

In a week, we were planning and making that suicide pact.

Alright, I know it's ridiculous and at the time I would have given anything that nothing would come about. But we were excited just talking about it, I can't tell you what a lift it gave us, that sense of purpose in our lives, even though it all sounds like bullshit now. Like I said, it gave meaning to our lives, like we were finally given an answer to why we were here.

We kept talking and Jimmy and I were soon in love. Real love. I know now it had always been there, since we were kids. Now, just like everything else, we could see it clearly, we put on those glasses that make everything clear in front of you. Everything that had been bottled up was coming out. It was beautiful.

I was careful with Kaz and his feelings. I didn't know this at first, but he and Jimmy went back to the dark ages, to first grade. Then Kaz and his family moved away for a long time, before moving back for Kaz's last year in high school. The more we talked, the more I could see why Jimmy and Kaz were so close. Kaz understood Jimmy more than anyone, more than Jimmy's own family, maybe even more than I did. I think Kaz loved Jimmy even more than I did. I was jealous of that, but I could live with it. As long as I still had Jimmy in some way. Just a piece of him.

Looking back, even knowing how everything turned out, I have to tell you that there was something about all this that made sense, like determinism, like Hegel's *Phenomenology of Spirit*, like a categorical imperative, like all that other philosophy bullshit. I have to believe that.

You tell me. Kaz studied engineering and already knew a lot about making explosives. Jimmy studied history and wrote a paper about European partisans fighting the Germans in the sewers during World War II. I studied urban design in New York and got to know everything about the city, even its subway and underground tunnels. You see what I mean. C'mon, pieces like that just don't come together on their own. Something besides us must have been putting us together all along.

We didn't know what to make of it. We didn't talk about it. What could we say? Sometimes you have to have faith that maybe there's more to everything out there than you think.

I never talked about it with Jimmy. It would've been all mystical bullshit, I was afraid I might lose him. But you know what I mean. We've all found ourselves in those situations, right? Where you believe that something more than yourself is at work, that something else is there behind the curtain.

Don't get me wrong, I'm taking full responsibility for what we did and what we got, but I'm just saying that I know there was something else at work here. I have to believe that, to make what happened worth it.

We were thinking the same thing and we were so fed up with The System and we talked about joining other groups and it was so clear that the only way we were going to do something was to get it done ourselves and suddenly we were swearing that we would do it, just the three of us, do something that could make some sort of difference, and that the only way left was through some kind of action, no more talk. You know those Ouija boards – when you were a kid, you would have your hands on the board and it would spell out something, something freaky – well, it was like that. Something wanted us to do it, and it knew that deep down we wanted to. It just gave us a little push.

Don't get me wrong. We weren't trying to start a revolution; we weren't trying to change The System, because we knew we couldn't change it. We hated it and we wanted to take a little bit of it apart before they caught up to us, and they would catch up to us. We had no doubt they would. We would just keep taking it apart until we were stopped. And we knew we were not going to be taken alive. We talked about that right from the start.

Jimmy said that at some point you can't care anymore, you reach the point of no return. You don't care about your life, only about the lives of others. Not just the ones closest to you.

At that point the way is made clear for you. The door opens. You just have to decide if you want to go through it. I haven't come close to reaching that point and I don't think I ever will. I don't think any of us will. But that night, when we made the suicide pact, we came pretty close.

It wasn't going to be easy, none of us thought it would be. We all thought we would die, and probably pretty soon, and probably not change a thing. I always just hoped that it would be quick, when the end came. I'm not good with pain, not like Jimmy, and not even like Kaz. We all agreed from the start that we would not go to prison, not let them humiliate us, or our families. What would be the point of living after we were captured? Think about it. What would we do in that kind of purgatory? We would just be living. The System could trot us out every once in a while, remind everyone how merciful it is because we're still walking around in our living death. No, we wouldn't let that happen.

We didn't want to hurt anyone, but we knew that was probably not possible, even then. We couldn't let it get inside us, feeling sorry for others, for ourselves, the questions, the doubts. That's residual crap from The System. Once it gets inside you, you're done. That's how they use it. The System is the moral law. We all wear invisible little ankle bracelets that keep us in line, tell us when we've gone too far. It makes you numb, unsure, until you have no fight left. It makes you want to go back to buying things, being a nice good citizen, living your life going from one mall to another, narcotized by TV. You want a purpose in life? We'll give you a family. All questions will be answered. Just channel all your doubts into that. All your emotions, all your thoughts, put it all into that family. Family becomes your church, your psychology, your purpose. The System loves families, the more the better, and families love The System. One big love fest.

That night was the revelation for me. Why wasn't I afraid? None of us were afraid. Not because we knew we weren't going to do what we said, but because we were going to do it. When we talked about our plan, I could see us, all three, dead.

It was so definite. And yet I wasn't afraid. Neither was Jimmy or Kaz. You can see why it was a miracle.

Looking back, I don't know why I was so interested in what was beneath New York City. It was weird, because I always hated dark places. I didn't know there was such a different world down there.

I did some urban exploring in my last year of college. One of our Profs recommended we learn more about the underbelly of the city. We were just about a bunch of bored college kids who thought it would be cool to become subway rats. There are people down there, some not so friendly, but not like in those movies with weird albino mutants with eyes that can see in the dark. And if those mutants are down there, thank God we never saw any. Now that I think of it, I don't remember that Prof ever going down there himself. Prick.

Most of us got tired of the dirt, filth and smells down there pretty fast. The majority never went down more than once or twice. I tried to get used to it, but never could. I lasted a little longer than most of the others. It's weird, some places in the tunnels are all noise and hell breaking loose, and there are places where you could be in some kind of shrine, water dripping, quiet. Nothing eerie at all. You could almost hear choirs.

Then there was all the organized stuff the three of us tried, separately. We tried the usual ways. Joined some socialist clubs in college. Went to meetings. Talked a lot. We could never decide on much. We went to those New York Occupy protests, Wall Street and others. Didn't even know all three of us were there. We got angry, like the others. Distributed pamphlets. Shouted at the pricks in suits. Got arrested. It was clear that nobody in those groups really wanted to change anything. They just wanted to meet and talk about it, and feel good about themselves being all involved and going to meetings and getting dragged off to jail for the night: a real inconvenience for The System. Then they would go home and get stoned and laugh at some capitalist reality TV. Try and get laid. They just wanted to feel above it all for a while before they sank into it, the family, the malls, the golf, all the activities that The System spins around them to forget that little glimmer of why they might really be here. Pretty soon they're the ones wearing the suits, getting yelled at, ducking into their offices, wondering where the fuck the police are.

The System loves these types. They're made for The System. The ones that go through the motions, find out what a mistake they've made, and get back into it with a vengeance. Truth is they've never left the fold. They're just born again, more fanatical than they could have imagined. The System needs these types to show everybody else that they're tolerant, wise and good, and, more importantly, don't hold a grudge. Leave them alone. They're not dangerous. Let them sink into it gradually. They won't even know they're drowning. You see how tolerant we are. When they come back, they'll be our strongest supporters.

There are so many ways out there to believe, to change, to make things better. All of them systems. That's just the way it is.

We learned soon enough that The System also needed us, maybe even more than any of the other radicals out there. It needed us as a warning that The System could also be a harsh and unforgiving parent to those who refuse to sink. It would show us how it dealt with disloyalty within the family. We played the bad seeds. It couldn't wait to get its hands on us. To show what happens when you spit in the eye of its kind indulgence. To show that The System is needed, that beyond it there's darkness and the unthinkable, whatever the hell that would be. They never say, do they, only leave it that way, mysterious and scary. Look at what these ungrateful few are doing, how they dare speak for all the others. We'll show how we deal with them.

There are criminals taken care of by The System. Millions of them. They're different. Most criminals don't want things to change, they're happy enough to try and use The System the way it is. The System loves criminals. Their failures give a moral blessing to what The System is all about. It can feed off the bogus morality that it's all about us, that The System only has our protection and best interests in mind, not its own.

For it is the law. The law, that metaphysical "forever" that hovers everywhere, treated like it is in our blood, in our DNA. No questions asked.

The more we talked about, it the more we trusted each other. Kaz and I even got to the point where we didn't hate each other. We could live with dislike.

We started to use The System like all the others. We became criminals to get what we needed to try and hurt The System later. Bring it down a little piece at a time, Jimmy said. And we really believed we could hurt it. Anything that strong and paranoid had to be weak, right? That's what we thought. That's what we told ourselves. I think we didn't really believe it even then.

I stayed with them in their apartment for the first few days. When Kaz was comfortable enough to trust me, they finally told me what they were up to. I was a little hurt that it took that much time for Jimmy to level with me. I had spilled my guts about myself from the start. I had nothing to hide. I wanted Jimmy to know everything about me, like it would bring us closer together, meld us together, create something that was only us – no longer him, no longer me, no longer separate – create an opening inside me that he could fill. Something that had nothing to do with Kaz. Only us. It hurt me a little that Jimmy held back.

They were working at a hotel in New York and they had already been planning against The System for some time. Then we were planning together. It went that fast.

We saved money, and studied the subway system, exploring the subway's tunnels and hidden secrets, moving everything in, until the day when we made those first killings. In revenge.

Any temptation we had to take our money and move to another city and start again, maybe even make a shitload of money – that never happened. At least not at the start. What would be the point? We would become the kind of people we wanted to bring down. I don't think any of us really thought it was a possibility. At least we never admitted it to each other. Not even with all the trouble that followed.

The hotel in New York was one of those boutique-y little twenty-room jobs with the faux cheetah-skin throws and film noir bullshit themes. All attitude, like it was real important stuff. The System loves places like this. Anything to keep you occupied, keep you moving along in the shuffle with everyone else.

They got me a job at the hotel – working in the laundry room.

Jimmy and Kaz had already been scamming credit cards off hotel guests. They had been doing it for a few months before I got there. They also had this prick, Vecchio, and some other fences set up by that time to move all the merchandise they could get.

The fences that we worked with never really trusted us. They were real. They liked nothing about us. It was always awkward. Real criminals can smell other criminals, real ones, they work in a comfort zone. Not with us. Even profit couldn't get them to get over their suspicion. I don't know what they thought of us. Fucking college kids. Working with the cops. I'm surprised we got out alive. We almost didn't.

At the end Vecchio wound up being the only one who would still work with us. I was always afraid of Vecchio. He was up to something. I could swear he figured out what we were doing. He was figuring an angle with us. He had those eyes. We tried to warn Kaz later on, but it was too late by then.

They wouldn't let me near Vecchio and the other criminals at first. It was only when they brought Vecchio around one time that I saw what kind of person we were partners with. I could see why they wanted to keep me away. There was no talk about what we were really up to at those times, only about using The System to make money. That was the only thing the fences would understand and that we could trust them with. We were both trying to fuck The System in our own ways. If we tried to tell them we were actually trying to kill it, we wouldn't have lasted a day.

The first thing I thought of when I saw Vecchio and his friends was that we had to do all this shit fast and get out with the money before we got way in over our heads with these people.

They were cold criminals. That's all. They were just as committed in their purpose as we were. Probably more. They were sure as hell dedicated to The System a lot more than some of the cops we met later.

I didn't like the way Kaz talked to Vecchio. Like he thought Vecchio was really cool. Only Jimmy saw Vecchio for what he was and you could tell Vecchio hated him for it. I didn't trust Vecchio from the very beginning. Here we were, using each other to make money, a necessary evil and all that shit. It was nothing but trouble.

I learned later that it was Vecchio who got the jobs at the hotel for Jimmy and Kaz. Vecchio had some family connections in the city. Jimmy became the assistant concierge and Kaz was brought in as a computer guy. We owed Vecchio too much right from the start.

I was told Vecchio's family owned part of the hotel but made sure they got a little more from their guests when they checked in and out. All I know is that Vecchio got fifty per cent of everything that we scammed. And I know that if it all came crashing down, Vecchio would serve us up in a heartbeat. We would have to be careful when that time came. And when it did come, it came a lot faster than we expected.

The Vecchio thing and the other fences were scary, but it was exciting, the whole thing about using The System to try and bring it down. We had to stay focused. Just us. We could only do it on our own. Win or lose, but it could only be us. No one else. Only that way could we last longer out there.

I told my mom after that first week with Jimmy and Kaz that I had a job in the city and would be living with them. She was really pissed at me for taking so long to get back to her, but like I said, we were moving a long way from our families by then. It was instinct. We were already trying to keep them away from all the trouble that was coming. I told her some bullshit that we were excited to be in the city and we would see how things go. She told me to make sure I visited often, to see her and my little brother. And if I didn't, to at least call. I cried at that point. I knew that I might not see her or my brother again. You never know. I couldn't try and look my brother in the eyes at that time. Children have that way of looking at you, knowing, right? That uncluttered clarity of innocence. I read that somewhere. They can see clearly that something is wrong. They just can't do anything about it. I didn't want to worry them even more.

In the end my mom thought I was just afraid to be in the city, away from home. I felt like I was betraying her and my brother with my secret. It was all I could do not to call Jimmy and try and bring him home again. It still wasn't too late at that time. Soon it would be. I got out of there fast, never looked back. I was afraid.

Like I said, I got a job, in the tiny hotel laundry room in the basement. I was the pleb. I didn't care. I was already underground at that point, like it was meant to be. It was a whole new world. You'd be surprised at what guests leave in their clothes when they're picked up for wash. Wallets, passports, all sorts of ID stuff. Hardly any of it made it to the laundry room. By that time most of it was taken by other staff. It wasn't hard for me to get some of it out, when it made it to the laundry room, there was no security in the basement.

Anything I got out to Kaz and Jimmy would be processed, money taken, electronics purchased and fenced, and the wallets tossed. At least that's how it started, but it became too risky and there wasn't enough of it to make it count. At least not compared to what Jimmy and Kaz were getting. I got caught second week taking a wallet from some guest's pants. I acted dumb, like I was just taking it out so the pants could be done, but it was the first time I noticed that the hotel did have a guy coming around every so often to check on the workers. It had its own little moral system and enforcement and was just as hypocritical, because it was fucking its guests a lot more than we were. It didn't mind what we were doing, it just didn't want us to get more than what had been arranged.

Because Kaz worked with the hotel security systems, he told me about a hidden camera that was behind one of the pylons near the laundry room and was almost impossible to see.

Kaz said that no one was really watching it, that it was a dummy camera. But something was up. I was afraid, more careful. I didn't trust anyone I worked with. Maybe there was more going on in this hotel than we knew.

The fact that I wasn't fired made me think that they weren't sure, or the family who owned the place was just going through the security motions, or maybe Vecchio was bullshitting us about the family all along. It didn't matter. The hotel had tipped its hand, and I never removed anything else after that. I decided to do things straight down there for the short time we had left. It wouldn't be long. That's what I kept telling myself.

Like I said, Jimmy and Kaz were the ones making the real money. Not all of it at the hotel.

There were a lot of ways to make money illegally, and not just with drugs. I got a quick lesson in how easy it was. Vecchio got his fifty per cent cut with everything we made at the hotel, but we got to keep everything else that we came up with.

It was a sweet setup at the hotel. Kaz hooked up a camera, a tiny little thing right over the registration desk, which would record credit card numbers. Kaz would be sitting in his computer room getting these ID numbers and then we would be ordering all kinds of stuff online. We had all the deliveries go to a house in Brooklyn that we rented early on. It was a small Victorian building in the Ditmas Park area of Flatbush. Mostly artist types and some cafes around. Nice area, where people were always getting things delivered. Food, electronics, new appliances, you name it. We didn't stand out. That's where the three of us sometimes lived while we planned.

Besides Vecchio and his people, we had a couple of other fences set up in Queens and other places on Long Island. Reliable people who could move the junk and get us a good cut. Better than what Vecchio was paying us. If Vecchio ever found out about it, we never heard anything about it. He would have done the same thing in our place.

It didn't matter. What kind of threat were we? To these fences we were just some young kids on the make, trying to use The System to get rich, just like them. Time-honored tradition, right?

We also had no doubt that if we tried to explain to them what we were really up to they would have thought we were crazy, reported us to the police or shot us on the spot. To these people, crackpot idealists are more dangerous than other criminals or police, any day. They understood trying to fuck with each other, but not with the cash cow. You squeezed The System a little, you didn't choke it to death.

Vecchio and these other fences must have been pretty surprised when we just disappeared one day. Maybe they thought we got in with even worse people, that we pissed off the kind of people that could actually make you disappear. It happens every day.

They had no idea what we were really planning. They thought we were just another bunch of criminals using The System to make money. Just like them. But they didn't know that we had something different in mind. I don't think Vecchio and the others ever really knew that all the shit that was all over the news, and that was yet to come, was because of us. At least they didn't know at the beginning. Until we became just another profit motive to that prick Vecchio. Just another part of The System he could profit from. Yeah, The System loves his type.

The hotel thing was temporary. We couldn't do it for too long. We all knew that. The hotel management and security were unbelievably dumb, but even they would put it together soon enough. No, we needed money, so we had to diversify our portfolio, as the suits like to say.

We had operations going on all over. I'm good-looking enough to get guys interested, especially after a few drinks at a night club. I got pretty good at lifting wallets. Probably could've been a pro.

This is how we worked it. Jimmy and I, we would get somebody in our sights, maybe a guy in his thirties or forties, you know the kind: an aggressive type A sales guy who had a few and is just shit-faced enough to have already pissed off several women by the time I come in, sit on his lap and pretend he's God's gift to our gender.

Then Jimmy comes in, acting all drunk, pretending I'm his girl. The bruiser always gets up to dispute the other Neanderthal's claim to his kill. Jimmy backs off, like he's the loser, and by then I have the guy's wallet, and I'm kissing him like he's my hero when he sits down again.

Then I'm off to the unisex restroom, slip the wallet under the next stall to Kaz. He has this cool little machine that scans the guy's ID stuff and then uploads it to his computer in Brooklyn. We usually had enough information right then to start buying shit online right away and sometimes a lot of shit because these guys had big credit limits. I'm talking carte blanche.

We only had a few minutes for all this to happen then I'd hurry back where the prick would be even more pissed and distracted. It was always easy to get the wallet back into his jacket.

Once, though, it went wrong. I mean really wrong. When I got back to the mark, he was standing there and I knew that he knew. He grabbed my arm but Jimmy came over and hit him. The wallet fell on the floor and we hurried out, got into our car and left. Then Jimmy sent a text to Kaz and Kaz coolly left the club and got a cab. That gig was done though. These nightclubs have a jungle communication thing set up with each other. We couldn't risk going back and trying it again.

We knew we had a limited amount of time to set it all up. Looking back, I can't believe how risky it was and how the fuck we got away with it. I mean, if we wanted to, and had we been thinking differently, we could have either become rich criminals or we could have ended up doing hard time in jail, there was no in-between. Some people are like that. Especially Kaz. That guy could have been lying on a beach somewhere wondering where he would get his next mojito. But Kaz wasn't built that way. Looking back now, I almost hoped he was. Maybe it could have ended differently if he had been just a cold-blooded prick, nothing more.

We knew all of this had a short shelf life. In the little time we had to make money we did everything we could, we even went dumpster diving near a rich kids' college to get their IDs and credit card information, we sold them fake IDs, we stole jewelry from hotel room safes, I even stole IDs from women shopping in department stores and supermarkets. You'd be surprised how many leave their wallets in shopping carts while they're nosing around the clothes racks or looking at the expiry dates for fillet mignon.

Kaz had this laminating machine in the basement of the house in Brooklyn. He made I don't know how many fake IDs for us and for those college kids. Realistic ones. Just in case. I'm glad I kept some. They came in handy later.

In three months we made about two hundred thousand, in a year we thought we could be at maybe one million dollars. I'm not kidding. That much. Except for the problem in the nightclub and the hotel room safe, everything else was so easy. I mean, if people knew just how easy it was being a criminal, using The System, I don't know how many would be doing it. The thing keeping most people back, like everything else in life, is fear, not any moral bullshit. Straight-up fear. Don't listen to that bullshit The System throws at you. It's always fear that keeps most people in line.

Well, alright, maybe it wasn't all that easy. After a while it became too risky. The police were starting to close in. One of our fences was arrested, probably the one who wasn't paying off the police. All I know is it wasn't Vecchio. The hotel had brought in a detective. Management suspected us. It was a matter of days. We had to get out. We were being set up.

We knew things were getting sketchy when Vecchio asked us to break into a safe in one of the hotel rooms. Some art dealer was staying at the hotel during a convention in town and he was supposed to be carrying a lot of cash which he put in his hotel safe when he went out.

Jimmy and I were against it, but Kaz had some macho thing going on, saying he was good enough to break into the safe and get the cash. It was Vecchio who put him up to it. Probably convinced Kaz that it would be really cool. Played on his vanity, that kind of thing. It was Kaz's blind spot. Everyone has one. Vecchio said it was only this one thing, this one time, but we knew that was bullshit. It's never just one time with these guys. Then Vecchio said that we had to do it, no more asking, that he was under pressure from other people. He owed them. And now he was threatening us, down the food chain, and just as we were planning to head out, Kaz came up with this idea that it could work.

It would be the last time we listened to Kaz. I didn't trust him much after that. Jimmy was going to tell him that this would be the last time, that we were leaving, telling no one where we were going, but then Jimmy decided not to at the last moment. There was something that ran deep with those two, always there under the surface, something that I could never really touch, something that made me angry because I could never get close to it. I was jealous because I sensed that it was something deeper than anything Jimmy and I would ever have.

Jimmy wanted to trust Kaz, we both did, and besides, it was Vecchio who was the real problem. He was getting more out of control and even more dangerous. It could have been all those drugs he was doing. After that night we were through with scamming The System. We had enough money put away. Kaz agreed. We would hold him to it. If he didn't do it, we would move without him. We would do this last thing, get a lot of money, and then we would disappear. Yeah. So simple.

Kaz got all the information on the safe, some Norwegian make, real complicated, he said. For Kaz to say that meant it was almost impossible.

A plan was put together. Some plan. Jimmy and Kaz were almost caught. They tried to open it one night when the dealer was out. It took a long time. But Kaz did it. And what do you know, there was nothing inside.

They barely made it out of the hotel before the police came. We met back at the apartment and I thought Jimmy was going to kill Kaz. Jimmy asked Kaz if he had told Vecchio about any of what we were planning, about The System, the secret plan. Kaz said no, but I don't know if we believed him anymore. Jimmy asked him if he had now gone too far with these scams and making money to go back to what we had originally planned. Kaz said no again, that he was never going to abandon what we had planned, but the truth is there had always been something there, that making money and buying things, that feeling with us, with the three of us, that was making us feel guilty. It wasn't just Kaz. That's what really worried us. It was making us drowsy, The System was, with its black magic. We were drifting away from our real purpose and we didn't even know we were moving.

I was glad about the way it turned out, this failure and betrayal by Vecchio. Maybe he didn't know the safe was empty, maybe he made a bet that Kaz couldn't open the safe with one of his friends, we didn't know and didn't fucking care. It was what we needed. A real wakeup call before it was too late and we were cruising the malls and sleepwalking like everyone else.

There was no choice now. We found out later that Vecchio knew that the hotel was onto us. He wanted us to get in a big hit before we were caught. He never told us anything about what was really going on. Never trusted us. It was only because I was taking a break from the laundry room, having a cigarette upstairs, that I saw the police come into the hotel and warned Jimmy and Kaz just before the police went up to the room. That prick Vecchio would have let them take the fall.

It gave us the feeling that maybe we had to think a little smaller about what we could do. And we tried, at least at the start. But we couldn't do it for long. I think each of us knew deep down that we would always go for the big kill in the end. It would always be all or nothing, couldn't be anything else. It had to be all or nothing with this kind of thing.

We were all for going to find that prick Vecchio, and I don't know what we would do to him, it was all talk, but that night it was all decided for us anyway.

We spent the night thinking about it at the apartment.

Then we went to a restaurant to talk about it. We had to get out of the apartment, but I was afraid someone would see us, hear us at the restaurant. But no one paid any attention.

That's the thing we noticed right from the start. That blind spot is a lot bigger than you might think. It's fear that keeps it small. After that night we agreed that we wouldn't hide or even disguise ourselves, that we would let it happen as it played out and let it end whenever it ended. Dead in one day or one year. It wasn't up to us. We would always move forward. That was the key. Move forward, don't hesitate, don't doubt. What's ahead is all that matters. That night we got all juiced up about it again.

That's when we swore the suicide pact to try and bring down as much of it as we could. We were all scared. We were still in our twenties and had agreed to die. What kind of fucked up shit that was. But it was real. And it almost stayed that way until the end.

It was that night, when we swore to the pact, that Jimmy told me he loved me. And I told him that I loved him. Despite my happiness I felt that we were saying goodbye, to lives that would never really begin. It was alright. It seemed so clear then. It was wonderful.

I remember how fast his heart was beating. He was afraid. I had never seen that before. It surprised me. I wouldn't see it again, not even at the end. We didn't say another word that night. I think Jimmy was afraid not because of what was to come, but because we knew there was no choice anymore. There was something at work that was beyond us. I think Jimmy felt it too by then. That's what scared us. There was another system at play here. And there was no way of tricking it. I think it was the first time that Jimmy really started to believe it. It frightened him, but it made us stronger and brought us closer.

The next day I was afraid that Jimmy and Kaz had called it off and we would all have a good laugh and go to a movie, get real. But they were just as afraid as I was. That's when we knew that something weird was at work here. Something else.

We all came up with different things. It just happened that way. I can't tell you what a feeling it is when life, even for a short time, becomes clear, and even though what you're going to do is scary, you know you're going to do it. Nothing else was possible. There was no point in even talking about it, because all three of us knew, we sensed, that in cases like this, talk was the enemy. There was no longer a why, only a how. It was a great fucking feeling. A cosmic feeling. And you know it's not going to last. That's what makes it more special.

We had this crazy theory that once you started thinking about it too much you were lost. Don't let your mind take over. Keep it off balance and it will tap into something more creative that will confuse the bigger System out there. Keep everything off balance. We were just kids, but we thought that maybe that was the thing that would keep us alive a little longer. The System doesn't understand stupid. Not in these situations. It was hard. But you'd be surprised how soon you start thinking this way. At a point, it just comes naturally. You might not even know you're doing it.

Alright, enough personal bullshit. It's just that to do something like this, it's not an easy decision, when you know you're going to die. You need a fucking good reason, right? It has to mean something. That's all.

It was time to go ahead with the plan.

The following night we vanished.

2

THE PLAN

We literally went underground. I'm not kidding. Underground. The subway is full of abandoned rooms and stations that connect with more buildings in the city than you could imagine. Many abandoned buildings, but also buildings that are still being used, have access to the subway via electrical rooms and basements, via parking garages, stairwells and maintenance rooms. This goes for all kinds of buildings.

Kaz found all this secret information about the subway that even the urban explorer groups didn't know about. He was like that, a master researcher. He could find anything.

I was proud that I knew a lot about the tunnels already. For a few weeks I felt like I was important, everything I knew was valuable to what we were doing. It was a great feeling.

We got to know the subway and the tunnels again. Really for the first time, because we were now looking for other things, anything that might help us live, at least a little longer.

What I learned is that the New York subway system has some weird tunnels running off it, like its own underground road system. A whole series of access and exit points, ventilation shafts and conduits that could get you into the strangest places, right into buildings with people working in them. You could get close enough to hear them. One time we looked in on a board meeting or something, real serious corporate types, and we started making these moaning sounds. They kept stopping and looking around. They had no idea what it was or where it was coming from. Maybe some of them thought the place was haunted, maybe others thought it had something to do with the ventilation. Finally the head honcho at the meeting left to call security and get some maintenance guys in, so we left.

You had to be careful. There was no real roadmap; you just had to feel your way around. Sometimes you can't see what's in front of you and you can fall through some rusted grate into a drainage system or get stuck in a narrow air shaft.

I remember there was a story going around that one of those urban explorers years ago fell into a hole under Fifth Avenue and died. When rescue people came in they couldn't find the body. The guy had just disappeared. Some of the explorers say that they've seen him with the mole people in the tunnels and he's now one of them. Maybe he's the one haunting the corporate building. Others say he was eaten by something weird that lives down there. That's how all this urban legend bullshit starts. That's the way we think, right? Even though we know it's all nonsense, it stays with us. All I know is that after that I was never as comfortable down there. You never know. At the end, I hated everything about those tunnels. After a few months we knew how to move around the city, both on the streets and below them. Except for the maps Kaz made, we kept as much of it as we could in our heads.

We were so excited. Fuck them. They wouldn't know what to make of us. Three young people in their twenties, from the suburbs, crazy enough to take on The System, not worried about money, things to buy, where to live, what teams were playing, everything we were supposed to worry about. No worry, The System would think, as soon as they got their new iPads they would be back in the fold. Fuck or be fucked.

No, they wouldn't suspect a thing. Just the sheer fact of our being there would make us invisible, make us that blind spot right in front of them.

Let them run around looking for Muslim terrorists. That's all they can think about now. It would never occur to them that it came from right here, right under them. Three young people from the suburbs. They would never believe it. They would never believe that The System had let three like us go.

They would always be looking for another system because they can't imagine existence without one. They believe we are systems. We are walking systems, we act like systems. All of us, living like those Russian nesting dolls, one system inside another and another. They understand this. Little else.

We would use anything, hunches, intuition, be as irrational as possible, anything but logic. Once you started using logic, you were playing their game. They would be three steps ahead, waiting for you. We had to keep them guessing, and the only way to do that would be to keep ourselves guessing, be as stupid as possible. It turned out to be not as hard or crazy as it sounds.

The only emotion we could never keep out completely was our old friend, fear. Fear was what kept us moving through those last few weeks. And then something else appeared. Something that made us vulnerable. Something that always happens. Something that makes you weak. Something you can never stop.

We're not the only ones who knew. The System can find places under the city, and not just under the city − it knows all these ways of going between buildings in New York. You wouldn't know all these buildings were connected one way or another, through their ventilating systems, through cable rooms, boiler rooms, you name it. There's a reason for that. The city doesn't want you knowing this. They don't want people coming into the city and running around beneath them and coming into board rooms and restaurants and crashing into fashion shows and concerts at Carnegie Hall. No, they keep it a secret and locked up like the crown jewels. But now we were opening those safes.

In a few months Kaz had a pretty good idea of how you can snake through these buildings, going underground and above ground, through as many blocks as you want.

He tested it a few times. In an hour he had worked his way around it like it was some Parkour event from a museum on West 22nd to an office building on 32nd avenue. Kaz came out through the parking garage on the third basement level, took the elevator up to the main level and walked through the lobby past the security guard and out onto the street, a quarter of a mile from where he started. He loved that route. He wrote it down for me on a little map, which I folded and kept.

Another time he made it all the way from West 23rd under Central Park to Fifth Avenue using an old discontinued subway line. He got into the tunnel through a maintenance door. He came out on Fifth through a basement in one of the swank townhouses across from the Museum of Art. Those places are always a lot easier to get out of than to get into.

One time he came out in the underground mall at Rockefeller Center, right into a group of tourists. Nobody looked at him or noticed him. Maybe a few of them. But nobody cared. That's the thing. Never forget that nobody cares. Not really. Not deep down. There's sympathy there, under all that crap that The System layers on top of us. Deep down most understand. Most want change. Any change. Then the fear kicks in. Who knows what's on the other side of that change. No, let's keep everything the way it is.

It didn't always work. Another time Kaz got lost and almost got stuck in a cable conduit and when he got out was in the middle of a sewer. He had to retrace to get back and got lost again. It took him six hours and when he returned to where Jimmy and I were waiting for him, almost shitting our pants, in the coffee shop on 52nd, he looked scared and messy like he had been thrown into a trash bin. He said he wouldn't go into the sewers again, but we knew that, if necessary, we would go anywhere to live a little longer. We didn't realize just how true it would be at the time.

Kaz being scared:, that scared me. I decided right then and there that if we were ever going to be in that same situation, we would be damn sure of the path we were going to take. No crawling through tight spaces, no sewers, no rats. I can stand on the edge of a forty-story building with all kinds of wind blowing, no problem. But no tight spaces, no constraints. I can't do it. The tunnels down there were too small for me. I didn't need any more nightmares.

I made sure that Kaz mapped out only places that you can easily get through. No crawling, no fear of getting stuck. My favorite was the way into the kitchen of a Chinese restaurant on East 34th Street through a ventilation tunnel. You could see the cooks in the kitchen through the ventilation grate. Kaz said that grate was so rusted that you could push it out, no problem, if we had to. These things you remember. You never know.

We planned the underground part for a long time, bit by bit. By the time we were ready we had set up living and sleeping rooms in seven different locations across the city. As far north as 194th, as far south as 3rd, as far west as the West Village, as far east as Stuyvesant Town. Like a military operation.

They're still there, if anybody wants to go see them. Why you would want to, I don't know. You can see the blankets and the food. My favorite was a little space we had made in the heating pipes above the parking garage beneath a building right in midtown Manhattan. It had enough room for two beds and I called it the tree house. It was warm and cozy and you had to stare really hard up into the pipes to see anything, even if you were right beneath our mattresses.

Jimmy's favorite was an old subway station under City Hall. You could only get to it through an abandoned maintenance tunnel. Jimmy liked it because there was a broken piece of stained glass hanging below the ceiling. If the light outside was just right it would come in and hit the glass and light up the painting of a little worker from a long time ago, maybe the 1920s. The worker's sleeves were rolled up and his arm was raised and he had a hammer in his hand, ready to come down. We couldn't tell on what. That part of the painting was all faded.

The little man reminded Jimmy of his father and brother. In happier times. We would eat in that spot a lot, as many times as we could, because it was dry and light and clean. There was light coming down through a vent, from the outside. It was like a little abandoned theater. If you listened closely you could just hear the traffic several stories above. Sometimes it even sounded like people clapping for that little worker.

I'll always remember that painting because it's where they caught up to us. It was the place Jimmy made his last stand.

Kaz was partial to a little space he found at the end of a long line of heavy wires in the utility room of a large condominium building off 27th Street. No one was ever in that room and it was always at about seventy degrees. The little storage cabinet was cramped but still large enough for the three of us to sleep there. Maybe it was like being back in the womb for Kaz, for all of us.

We had four other sleep locations across the city, and eight places where we stored canned food and water, just in case we had to become long-term moles. By the end we had three locations of stored weapons, including guns, ammunition and chemicals to make explosives. I hated those rooms because of the smell of the chemicals. It was worse than the chemistry lab at school. It made Jimmy sick. Those rooms were Kaz's domain. I only went once into one of those rooms. We called it the bomb shelter, because that's where Kaz brought in the chemicals to make the explosives.

It was an odd-looking space, the bomb shelter. It looked like an orphan room that served no purpose, probably left over from when they were building this section of the tunnels. It was all concrete block walls and a dirt floor, the ceiling so low you could just stand upright. There was no door, and when Kaz was making his explosives Jimmy and I had to be far away down the tunnel before Kaz would start. We hated those times. We always waited for the blast in silence, looking away from each other. Maybe because part of me was hoping for it, I don't know, maybe that's why Jimmy and I couldn't look at each other. Maybe he sensed what I was feeling. That I hated myself for it.

We also brought in some medical supplies, not much, but at least it was something.

I don't think anybody ever found any of those rooms and supplies. Maybe I'm wrong, I don't know. Maybe they're still waiting there for someone to make any sense of it. The System doesn't need to know or care.

Over the weeks when we were still working at the hotel, we visited pharmacies, paint stores, and chemical supply shops to buy all the ingredients we thought we would need to make the bombs. A little bit here and there. We were patient and didn't attract attention. Gradually, our store of materials for making bombs grew. So did the odd names that Kaz was throwing at us, names like tetra nitrate, potassium nitrate, other names I can't remember.

By the time we were ready, we had some good maps of the New York subway tunnels, Kaz had information about explosives, and Jimmy showed us something else, an automatic pistol. That was when it really started to sink in for me. Seeing that gun. The explosives and chemicals were strange and remote, somehow. The gun made it all closer and real. At first I hoped we would never have to use the guns. Now I laugh when I think about it.

We bought more guns and learned how to use them.

It was easy enough through Vecchio. He could find almost anything for us. Kaz dealt with Vecchio the most. I found out later just how close Kaz got to Vecchio, how he told him things that he shouldn't have. Jimmy and I stayed away from Vecchio, we only dealt with him a few times, only when we had to, but Kaz became friends with him.

That was something that would catch up to us, and not just that night at the hotel. Thing is Vecchio knew things about the three of us that he shouldn't. Things that would matter later. Now I think of it, he must have known what we were up to almost from the start. He was a shrewd prick. That we'd all regret. Funny, Vecchio was always saying that he would get his big reward, he wanted his big reward. Maybe one day he would get it. I hope the fuck he will.

Kaz was the explosives man, but after some time I wanted to learn too. Then we all had to learn. I had a mask to cover my mouth and after some time I got used to the chemicals. So did Jimmy. In a few weeks we were all good enough to make some kind of bomb that actually worked without killing us. I took good notes about everything that Kaz said about explosives.

I was scared about the whole thing. Terrified. I kept telling myself that it didn't matter when death came, because it would come. It didn't help with my nerves. I just hoped I could at least get something done before I blew myself to pieces.

I don't know what drove Kaz to make another kind of bomb. It was something to do with cellphones, something he said he shouldn't be doing, that it was using technology we said we would avoid, and we shouldn't tell Jimmy about it. He only showed me for a few moments how to detonate it using another cellphone, and then he put it in a paper bag and hid it. He told me it should be used only when absolutely necessary. If used on the surface it could be traced. In the tunnels it didn't matter, there was probably no way of picking up a signal or using the cellphones to set if off anyway. I remember it was an old cellphone that he took apart with a small plastic package beside it and some wires in between. It was all together on a small piece of plywood with metal clips and those thin plastic zip ties for holding things together. It looked like something a kid would put together in science lab at school. It looked harmless enough. Maybe Kaz was just playing a stupid joke on me.

He was serious enough. He gave me the other old cellphone and told me to hide it, and never turn it on until the explosive would be used. I put the cellphone in a duffel bag and forgot about it.

I don't know why Kaz made it and why he told me about it. Maybe he knew I would need it one day. I don't know about these things, but I knew I would never mention it to Jimmy, even though I hated keeping secrets from him. Something told me not to let Jimmy know. In the end it didn't matter anyway.

3
LOOSE ENDS

Once we did what we did, there was no turning back. I think that we did it so that we couldn't go back. It was done. Bridges burnt, right?

We still had to get some personal stuff out of the way first. It was always there, in the back of our minds, that we would do what we did, even though we didn't talk about it. We just knew we would do it, because if we didn't, nothing else was possible. That's what we believed, without talking about it. It was a test, you see. And it changed us. Because we knew there would be no going back.

We said goodbye to our families in our own way. We said goodbye without them knowing it was goodbye, one Sunday.

I knew that was the last dinner I would have with my mother and little brother. I don't think they suspected anything. I'm not sure. They thought I was just quiet. To my credit I didn't cry. Just once. I went to the bathroom and got it under control.

Maybe my mother just thought I was having a hard time with Jimmy. It wouldn't have been the first time. At the end we all hugged and my mom asked if everything was alright and I said yes and she left it at that. She sensed that something was about to happen. I swore to myself that whatever would happen I wouldn't get them involved. They would know nothing. We said goodbye and I promised that I would be over again soon. She always knew when I was lying. I couldn't look at my brother. I was afraid of what I would see in his eyes.

Jimmy and Kaz said goodbye to their families in their own way. All I know is that when we met later at the apartment in Queens, we were quiet and we had made as much peace with what we were going to do as possible. Everything was like a new starting line for us. We just had to cross it and not look back.

We made sure we couldn't come back. Before we disappeared for good, we had to settle some scores.

The first one was the bank manager who fired my father. That happened sixteen years ago, when I was eleven. My father was an assistant manager at a small bank in New Jersey. He was fired and told to leave immediately and was escorted from the building. Like a criminal.

My family was never sure why he was fired. All I know is that my father shot himself a few days later.

Sixteen years later, we got the bank manager in the parking lot of the same bank branch. I couldn't pull the trigger. In those few seconds that I hesitated the bank manager pulled a gun from his coat, can you believe it? The prick would have shot us if Jimmy hadn't gotten his gun out and quickly nailed him three times. The weird part is he didn't even look surprised, like he was waiting to be taken out. Like we did him a favor. Who knows how many others he had fucked over the years. Maybe it was his redemption time.

We ran and we knew then that this was it, there was no turning back. It was almost a relief, that fucked-up kind of relief you feel when you know there are no other choices. This is it. This is what you deal with now. We were almost giddy with relief.

We had to be fast. The System would have already noticed and would be moving towards us. We found the foreman who laid off Jimmy's father and older brother at the metal machine shop. I don't know how many years ago this had happened, but I know Jimmy's father had worked there a long time.

It fucked up Jimmy's family. Jimmy's father was too old to find another job. He smoked and drank himself to death. Jimmy's brother had to find work at a meat plant and died when he was cut by one of the machines and the tainted meat got into his blood.

Sure, you can look at it from I don't know how many angles. Jimmy's father and brother had to go, right, because it made some kind of economic sense. Yeah, nothing fucking personal. You think that way, then they have you, might as well have stuck a tube in your head and fed you capitalist pablum right from the start.

No, you still might say, hey, the foreman has a job to do, he has a family, he can't be responsible for what happens after he's fucked these people. That's out of his control, out of his hands. Their responsibility, someone else's responsibility, maybe his boss's, maybe blame that old standby, fate. You think that way, you're good and fucked, they should make you a statue, capitalist fuck of the year. Because they have you coming and going, every moral and philosophical angle covered. No problem. They don't even have to talk, you're already doing all the talking for them. You're a capitalist shill and don't even know it. Right this way.

No, The System's always telling us that we have to be responsible for our actions, right? Alright then, it was time for a payment long overdue.

Somewhere along the line there had to be some responsibility. A reckoning. We started with the personal ones.

It was time to settle.

The foreman was an old guy. He wasn't like that bank manager prick. But he, too, surprised us. We wouldn't have figured that he was the one who would beg for mercy, but he did. We walked right into his fake wood-paneled office when he was on the phone. At first he screamed at us and threatened us and got up and tried to puff himself up real big and scary, and jump up and down, I mean what an asshole, probably treated everyone that way. No, maybe not everyone. I'm sure he's real nice with his bosses. At first I wasn't sure I could go through with it again. And then he started with the big ape routine, right in our faces. That changed everything.

You can't hesitate. We learned that real quick. If you forget what you're dealing with here even for a few seconds, they'll kill you. They'll use anything to survive. They're programmed to deceive and use anything against you. They can't think any other way. They're just a reflection of The System.

He whimpered when he saw the guns. My family, my family...please...yeah, it's OK when it's *his* family. Like I said, they'll try anything. I plugged him four times. The big slab of meat turned, did a little ballet pirouette like the hippo in that jungle cartoon and fell flat on his desk. All hell broke out. Unfortunately Jimmy had to shoot a security guard on the way out. We found out later that he was OK.

It really bothered me later. We had nothing against that security guy...but why did he have to go and draw his gun at $6.50 an hour? That's how The System fucks people up. Sometimes the people most screwed by The System become its biggest defenders. You ever notice that? What kind of weird psychology is that? This security guard could tell that we weren't there to rob the place, we didn't have any bags with us, we had nothing against him and the others at the company, that was obvious. He probably knew this foreman was a conniving prick, treated him like shit. Probably had visions of plugging the bastard himself. Why would we walk into that place and shoot somebody and walk out if the guy we shot didn't deserve it in some way?

No, this is his job, fucking right or wrong. Instead of walking away, he comes running in, his gun out, the moral defender. Dedicated protector of the status quo. God bless The System. If Jimmy hadn't been such a good shot by then I would have been dead beside that foreman.

We didn't run this time. We walked out of the building and strolled to our car in the parking lot. We had to try it, we had to see if it would work. No one followed us, no one shouted at us. They might have even been saying a little prayer of thanks. Who knows. I remember I was very calm, but my hands were shaking. It was weird. Kaz drove and Jimmy put his warm hands over mine and they stopped shaking. That's when I knew there was no turning back. We were fucked, but we were fucked together.

By then we were on a roll. The next one was for Kaz. The insurance company executive who refused to pay for Kaz's mother's medical treatments. We knew this one was going to be a treat. Kaz's mother died a year after she was refused treatment. A slow, miserable decline into death. How Kaz found the executive was nice. He took his time, got to know someone at the insurance company, and eventually saw the signature of the one who put a big rejection stamp on the whole thing.

We almost forgot with the foreman and the banker. Almost paid for it. We wouldn't let that happen again.

It was a woman and she was a doctor. Can you believe it? So much for the gentler sex. We came up to her just as she was getting into her car and ended her with three shots. One from each of us. I'd like to say that we were more creative, that we used a syringe with an exotic chemical, her being a doctor, but there just wasn't time for it. That shit is for the movies. We didn't even talk to her. She didn't even see who was about to kill her. She wouldn't know us anyway. She didn't even have time to be surprised. One second she was there, the next gone. We walked back to our car like we had just picked up something from the supermarket. It was like we had an invisible bubble around us, we could see everyone else but they couldn't see us. No one followed us, no one knew or seemed to care.

We never found out much about these people. Just who they were, their names and where they worked. We didn't want to know if they had families, if they attended church, were good neighbors, played bridge with their buddies, mowed their lawns, prayed for the good of humanity. We didn't want to know. They never gave a fuck about us or the rest of our families. Why should we give a fuck about them and their families? They went on, business as usual. We just did the same.

Don't let them engage you in their conversations. That's when everything bogs down, gets fuzzy and confusing. You see it all the time in the movies. The thing is, it's true. Delay enough and something's going to happen. They'll play on your emotions and try to get in your head. That's what we were up against. The System will do anything to win, to survive, why should we expect anything else from people made by the same system? That's when they have you, when you hesitate, when you question yourself and what you're doing. When you're not sure, then you're fucked.

Truth is, The System wouldn't hesitate. It would crush you, no questions asked. It's always devious. It has so many options to go to, to play on your sympathy, your good nature. They'll tell you that it's all evolution, all social Darwinism, these fucking Darwinists will tell you that it's in our blood and genes, and all of us are programmed to do anything to each other to survive. Anything. We were to find out soon enough how much of that was true.

No, that's just an excuse for the people who benefit from it. That's what they want you to believe: that The System is only a reflection of what all of us are really like deep down. Nothing more. But there is more. I have to believe that.

Don't think we got used to the killing. It didn't happen. At first there was that sense of relief, that sweet feeling that the choice has been made, no going back. But it didn't last long. I was numb for days after it. We didn't talk or eat. Jimmy and I came close to breaking up. The only thing that kept us together was the idea that what we did was right. Necessary. It was best to be around each other, because we shared something important. We didn't feel good about it. But we knew it was necessary. In a funny way, after a few days, it made us surer about what we wanted to do. Then it brought us closer. No, there was definitely no turning back now.

From then on, we were on the run. Our faces would be all over every traffic cameras' footage. The System would now be gathering the evidence, screaming revenge and rounding up the forces to find us. It doesn't care about those people who were killed. It only cares about the fact that it had been disrespected. The System is as vain and sensitive as a prom queen. Everything it can't control is an insult to it. Well, screw it. Let them come.

We never had any intention of hanging around and playing games anyway. There was too much more to do. The killings made it impossible for us to do anything else than what we were going to do. There was no other choice.

That same night, after we killed the doctor at the insurance company, we went into the subway and disappeared from the world.

I'm sorry if I'm done with soul-searching.

You might be thinking, when you're reading this, "what cold-blooded bastards!" If you do, then you know they have you. Give me a chance and I'd be thinking the same thing in a few years. Come near my kids or property and I'll kill you. I'd probably be one of The System's biggest supporters. Emotions and morality are two big weapons for them. It's one of the ways The System keeps you in line.

How dare they presume to judge what's better for everyone! That's what you're thinking. And it's here that The System's moral outrage and belief in itself is scary. You can't get any more self-righteous. There's no middle ground given. No, if you want to try and change it, it's all or nothing.

From the beginning we kept that small apartment in that old building in Queens, where the gangs were scarier than the police. We never felt comfortable there. That neighborhood had its own system, just as hostile to outsiders as any other. Everybody watched us.

As for that house in Brooklyn, that's where we kept most of the equipment we needed. That's where Kaz kept his laminating machine, all the equipment we bought and fenced. Before we started, Kaz made up a few extra ID cards for us, using the machine. It was mostly for his ego, to show us how good they were, and they were good. We didn't think we would need them. I still have a few in my pocket. Even now. You never know. Fake names – it all seems so funny now. Nothing could have been as unreal as the life I was living then. It all seems so unreal now.

I said before that, from the start, we decided to go the opposite way from what you'd expect. What they would expect.

The only technology we allowed ourselves were some watches, not even digital, just analog.

If we had to go into the tunnels, we figured we couldn't communicate with cellphones anyway. The police can trace them no problem. Terrorists have all the latest technology, right, the police would be expecting it. We would be quiet, move under the radar. If we used cellphones, it was only because we had to, and there was no other way. Funny, it was what really got us into trouble at the end. We had the right idea. We just couldn't execute it.

No computers to do research on bombs, on the subway and tunnels, on anything. They can trace anything now, as far back as they want. Nothing has given The System more ammunition than the internet. It's been able to absorb the net into itself. You know what I mean? All this talk about social networking and the freedom of the net, don't believe it. They all think they're operating outside it. The System lets you think that, and all the time it's there, all around us. We've all just sunk into it.

We wouldn't wear disguises, wouldn't worry about security cameras. We would be right out there in the open. Not that we were trying to get caught. Just trying to find The System's blind spot. That's what Jimmy called it. The System had a blind spot, like most things, like cars do when you're on the highway. A car could be only a few feet from you, right beside you, and you wouldn't know it. We were trying to get as close to The System as we could, without getting run over by it. Kind of like those little fish that hang on the backs of sharks, out of sight, away from those teeth. That was the theory. We hoped Jimmy was right about it. We knew we wouldn't have a lot of time to test it.

Like I said, we decided early on that we couldn't live. That we didn't want to live. We didn't want to be all over the media, we didn't want The System to be gloating about us. We didn't want our families to be looking at us, ashamed. In a few months we would be forgotten anyway.

It was simple enough, we decided. Learn about explosives. That was the most important thing. We used a small field out in the middle of nowhere in Connecticut to test our bombs. Only small charges, because we didn't want to attract attention. Two small explosions and then some kids showed up on bikes, staring at us. We left in a hurry. There's no place away from people. Not really. The System has eyes everywhere. It doesn't need CCTV. People will report anybody to protect The System. They're happy to do it. They feel like it's their duty. I'm not kidding.

After that we found another spot to train with our handguns. Inside the tunnels under the city. Right under the watchful eyes of the painting of the worker with the hammer. It was perfect. All the old equipment and tools lying around helped deaden the sound.

We barely learned how to use our guns, and we agreed to kill ourselves before we were taken. It was easy enough to get the guns from Vecchio. Criminals, even petty ones like our fences, all had them and just thought we needed them for protection. Jimmy gave me and Kaz small nine-millimeter Glocks. I didn't know where to put it, so I kept it in my backpack. We read manuals about the best spots to stop or kill a man, targeting the chest area and the head. It almost made me sick.

As soon as I saw those guns, and started using them – they were so real and hard and they were only meant for one thing – I knew I wasn't cut out for this. I'm no revolutionary. I don't know what I am, but I do know I thought that I couldn't fire that gun if it came to that. Jimmy knew it. It was nothing that I said, just the way I looked. He told me that if it came to it, I wouldn't need a gun. He would protect me. I felt the same way until we got to that foreman that screwed my family. Then I couldn't stop firing. I think we're all a little surprised at what we can do when it comes down to it.

It was always a scary thing with the guns. None of us really knew what we were doing at first. I don't know how we didn't kill one another. We found an old FBI training manual in the library in Queens. We practiced reloading our pistols for a long time, until it was easy.

We learned to load our guns fast, without looking at them or our hands or the magazines.

We learned to emergency reload, when you've spent all the rounds from your magazine and the slide on your gun is locked back. We learned to do this while we kept our guns pointed at our targets. You see, the manual said lowering your gun gives your target an advantage over you and keeps you focused on your gun instead of on your target. All the time you're loading a fresh magazine into your gun. Yeah, sure. Easy, right? I never thought that I would use it, until I had to.

We got to be practiced enough that when we were shooting, no matter how many rounds were in the magazine, we were able to feel when the handgun was empty. Not bad. And we got good at firing when moving. Not easy.

We even practiced something called the Mozambique Drill. I'm not kidding. It's not a dance. It's a real thing. This is how it worked. Kaz would call out target numbers, and if he called the number of a target you've already hit, this time you go for a head shot. Why? Maybe the target is on drugs, wearing body armor, or really fucking mad and crazy, and he keeps coming at you. That's when you have to take the headshot.

There was other weird stuff in the manual. Like even if you destroy a person's heart they can still have almost half a minute of life left to try and kill you. No shit. That's what it said.

The manual said that in an intense situation you will not do anything you have not practiced. I was to find out later this wasn't true at all. Not for me. It was all bullshit. When the time comes, you run on instinct. That's it.

The craziest and scariest drill of all was charging at someone who has a gun and is trying to reload or is distracted, it didn't say by what. The trick is to try and catch them off guard. The manual said to head towards the target, slow down to a crouched walk with your knees slightly bent to keep your upper body smooth, and then shoot the target while he's still reloading. Yeah sure. I hoped that I would never have to try this one, I mean for real. That went for any of them.

How stupid we must have looked with all these amateurish moves, down there under the city. At one point we heard someone laughing, a little child. It was the girl I had seen earlier in the tunnels, with the mole people. It must have looked so funny to her. She ran away when we saw her. At first we were embarrassed and then we tried to find humor in what we were doing.

But it made us worried, just how silly we must have looked. Even a little girl couldn't take us, or what were we doing, seriously. I hated the guns. After three more practice sessions I told Jimmy and Kaz I couldn't do any more.

What was the point? When my time came, I would probably freeze. The gun was as useless as a water pistol in my hand. I had better luck with the explosives. There was something faraway about explosives, even though I was scared shitless when I was helping Kaz make them. Making bombs was like solving a puzzle. It's all about the head, putting the right pieces together. And when they went off and made that awful noise, it seemed so distant, harmless. Not like the guns.

What kinds of revolutionaries are afraid to kill, to do what's necessary? We're cowards. Do you really want to hear about that? Do you want to hear about cowards, incompetent idiots? No, we had to be more than that.

I was ashamed. Who were we? Three fools in way over our heads. If we had any sense, we would have left right there. We still had a chance to get out. No harm done. But we didn't. We stayed in. Something made us stay in. We thought we could play a little bit, then leave. Idiots.

That was before we settled those scores for our families. It was exactly what we needed. It became easier to kill after that, even if we didn't want to. After that the guns were no problem for me.

I know now that the guns were never the real problem for me. Not really. It was something else, something bigger. It's easy to forget about what you're doing, I mean the real reason you're doing it. You ever ask yourself that? It was the same with us. We had to talk about it, keep our anger and juices strong, or it became like any other job, boring, and you could find yourself drifting away from the real purpose. We kept talking about our enemy, The System. That kept it alive for us.

Almost everyone works for The System one way or another. The System always tells you it's for your own good. It relies on your self-interest, the protection of your private property, the fear of chaos and anarchy. We were always laughing about these flag-wavers, these patriots who cry when they hear the national anthem and who would fuck you in a second if you got anywhere near their precious property. Those people are the best people for The System, and those are the people who don't even know that they're in fact working for and worshiping The System, not their country. They become slaves to The System, its eyes and ears; they consider it their patriotic duty. The System doesn't have to do any selling, any convincing; it has already been done for it. The best marketing and PR available. For free.

No wonder The System puts on the big patriotic displays for its people. It needs them as much as they need it. Feed the frenzy. The biggest myth is that this country is run by its people, almost everyone believes that. Unh-unh, The System runs the country. It couldn't give a shit about the people. It's way past that point. It needs them to survive, that's all. And anything that it believes will pose any kind of threat to it will be dealt with harshly. The System lives only for itself. It doesn't give a shit where it lives, as long as it lives. It just happens to be living in what is called America. But it'll move wherever it can survive.

We talked about it in the apartment, in the house in Brooklyn, in the tunnels, in a restaurant, we didn't give a fuck who was listening. Everything out in the open. We had no illusions about what we could do. It was a suicide mission. All we knew was that we felt we had to try and do something. We knew we were already talking too much.

The problem is The System loves talking; it'll keep everyone talking for as long as it can. It stopped listening a long time ago. It loves it when its people tell each other to go through the proper channels if they want to make any changes. Proper channels will never change or hurt it. They will only bring in more supporters. Make The System stronger.

We decided to try and be different from the start. None of us are leaders. We can barely make up our minds about anything. We're not followers. And we're not joiners. Maybe that would help confuse The System, we didn't know.

Truth is The System was used to dealing with people who are slotted into the proper, expected channels. People who join large movements and protests, who try and make changes through politics, who join radical parties or terrorist groups, who join systems. This it understands too well. This it can deal with, can contain the problem, track it and kill it or absorb it and make it part of The System itself.

But maybe The System wouldn't know what to do with us. It didn't care why we were doing it. It didn't care about that. It couldn't understand how we were doing it. We're not computer hackers, we're not organized terrorists. Maybe there was no category for us. Maybe we could slip between the cracks. I smile now when I think about it. Real idiots.

Time was also important. Wait too long and we fall into the usual pattern, maybe get married, maybe have children, maybe buy some property, maybe hustle in our jobs, maybe try and get our kids into great schools, maybe, maybe… and soon our world shrinks and soon enough we don't give a fuck about anything else but our kids and our own property anymore, and we're out there waving flags like everyone else, and patting each other on the back and crying when the national anthem comes on. Oh yeah. Welcome to The System.

You can see them walking around, ex-radicals who have come to terms with The System, been absorbed by it, that have given up, whatever. Old vegetarians, growing organic shit, maybe going to the occasional protest, still thinking they're making a difference, making changes, coming to terms with how to do things, going through those proper system-blessed channels, when they don't even realize they became part of what they're trying to change a long time ago. They're like strange sad sleepwalkers who have been lobotomized, harmless. It's easy to do, you don't even know it's happening. You can't see because there's nowhere left to look now. No, that wasn't going to happen to us.

The System wants to keep everyone divided, old and young. It wants the rift. It uses music and other media to keep them even more apart. It wants disdain for old people, because it can control young people, it feeds off their energy and it grows stronger. The System wants to keep old people on the sidelines, feeble and used up, so even if someone had something to say, from all those years of wisdom, no one will listen. They're only used up, empty shells. Most don't have anything to say, they only spew out little pieces of wisdom about how to live and die within The System, just like they do. That's the conceit of old age. Most want their children to be a better version of themselves. The System loves it. It's the best marketing for it. It doesn't have to pay a thing. It has all generations safely in its pocket. Everything already paid up in full.

It was all strange. Explosives and guns. I began to see underground New York as our burial place. I had nightmares about it at first.

4

UNDERGROUND

We hated the tunnels at first. We would try and stay out of them as long as we could. Down there was dark and wet, and there were weird sounds. There were things that liked living in the dark. I think we were afraid that the longer we stayed in the tunnels, the weaker we would become. We were afraid that we wouldn't have the strength to continue, or to even leave those tunnels.

But things began to change, I don't know why. There was a peace down there that I didn't notice at first, none of us did. It could be calm down there, if you didn't fight it. Funny how we only noticed it after we had resigned to our fate.

This was after that time, and I will get to that, when we tried to get out, tried to escape, just before we realized how impossible that would be. By then it was too late. That's when we found ourselves at peace with what was about to happen, and at peace with the darkness. I never knew it could be so beautiful. Even the dreams became beautiful.

We swore that there would be no killing in the city, that we would be careful about it. We had done enough killing on the surface. What I didn't know was how easily people die, even if you don't want them to, even if you plan really carefully.

We really tried. We would target buildings, not people. Buildings that we believed stood for the most hated part of lives out there, at least in our own eyes. You know what I'm talking about. Banks and corporations, the biggest blood-suckers out there.

We had to be careful from the start. Once we entered the underground tunnels, it meant that we were on the run from everything out there.

As I said, going off the grid was important. No cell phones, television, newspapers, credit cards, IDs. Nothing that could be traced. Nothing to distract us or trip us up. Why make it any easier for them? This was hardest for Kaz. He was the techie and for him it was like breathing, like an addiction. In the end, we should have been harder on him about it, but what do you say to a friend in that situation? It was only a matter of time before we were dead, and survival was out of the question. A few more days don't really matter, right? We finally let Kaz use his electronics. When it came back to screw us, we didn't say anything. It would have happened anyway, and we knew it.

We also said that we would do as much in the open as we could. We believed that if we tried to hide everything, tried to be as careful as we could, we'd be caught right away. It's what they would expect, it's what they would be watching for, what their whole strategy was about. Everything, everything in the way they hunted was geared towards searching the dark corners, the places where we would be expected to hide, always on the run.

No, we would do it another way. We didn't care about the security, we would stay in the open, we would be as casual as possible, business as usual. No masks. Grinning right at the cameras. Here we are.

They would look right past us, wouldn't even notice us standing in front of them. It wouldn't even register, because they couldn't imagine reality being anything else than what they thought it would be, just like those philosophers said a long time ago. It's all in the mind. At least that was our theory.

It was Jimmy's idea, and we could see where he was coming from. It's just hard to do it. Put theory to work, you know. Especially when you're testing it on something like The System. Like throwing a rock at a sleeping lion then running straight at it as it's running straight at you. Like the drill with the guns.

Run straight at him. You get the idea. As crazy as it gets. But maybe crazy would keep us alive longer.

Like I said, we didn't go into the tunnels right away. We wanted to stay above ground as long as possible, in the apartment, until that all changed.

We might need these places if we had to go above ground to get away from the authorities, or if we just needed a change. Don't get me wrong, some of the places in the tunnels are alright, even beautiful. I mentioned the old train station already. There's another spot, near a maintenance tunnel, where a little light comes in from somewhere, and when the light is just right it lands on part of the old brick and right on another old painting. It's hard to make out now, much of the paint is gone, but you can still see the outline of a young woman's head. She's staring at the maintenance tunnel, like she's waiting for someone. Maybe for the worker in the other painting, at the old station. She has been down there a long time, keeping her secret, just like we were trying to keep our secrets.

Kaz would go back every so often to sit and stare at the painting. Who did it? Maybe someone like us, hiding down there because he had done something just as stupid as what we were about to do? There was no signature. What was the point? There was no one to see it. No one to know what the artist had left behind.

This is where we found the little girl who would later become important to us. She had come to see why people like us had entered her dark world. To see if we were friendly, or crazy. Friendly could be scarier down there than crazy, any day. It would be some time before she learned to trust me. In the end I think I was the only one of us she would trust. I would see her sometimes looking at the face of the beautiful woman in the painting. So out of place here under the city. I never found out what the girl thought of the painting, whether she believed it was her mother, maybe an angel, maybe both. I know I would have in her situation. Sometimes you just need to believe.

Like I said, there were some beautiful places, but there were also things that crawled in the dark, and not always animals, and there were the filth and the smells.

We tested how long we could last down there.

I had to go and shower at the apartment after one day. Jimmy and Kaz lasted a little longer, but not much. Not as long as the people who live down there. We had seen maybe twenty of them over the weeks. They were good at leaving us alone and we sure as hell didn't want to attract more attention than we had to.

We knew the spots of these people, where they sleep, and we avoided them as much as we could. As long as we weren't interested in their territory and weren't crazies going down for sport to kill a few of them (they told us later that it happens, that's how sick some people can get), they couldn't have cared less about what we might have been doing. Later, we regretted not getting to know these people a little more. If we had, things might have turned out different. I don't know.

We avoided the tunnel people as much as we could. The only time we almost got involved was when we saw a couple of drug dealers kicking the crap out of one of them. For no reason. We thought about helping the poor old guy, but stayed away. I hate to say it but it was near one of our lab rooms, where bombs were made, and that was just as much of a concern as the poor old guy, maybe more. And we thought we might draw too much attention. It was hard to watch. They beat him to death and walked away, laughing. These are the kinds of pricks The System produces. We let them go. The other mole people came back when it was clear and looked at the old guy then left him there. They saw us, I'm sure they saw us, and they saw that we did nothing to help. They would have never trusted us after that.

Next day the body was gone. Either the mole people had a way of dealing with their dead down here, or the tunnels somehow did. It made the tunnels even creepier to me.

I did get to know that young girl who lived with some of the older women down there. She couldn't have been more than twelve or thirteen. I never learned her name. She knew a lot more about the tunnels than we did. She must have been down there for a few years. I gave her some of my clothes and one time, when she was sick with the flu, we gave her some of our medicine. She got better.

Kaz and Jimmy didn't want to get too close to her and the others. They never really trusted them in the first place. But I knew the girl was OK.

The girl did warn us about subway maintenance men. We never saw many over the days we were down there. The ones we saw were loud and easy to avoid. The tunnel system is big. You can go a long time down there without seeing anyone, if you know your way around, and that's what you wanted to do.

I cried the first night in the tunnels. I didn't want Jimmy or Kaz to hear me. I tried to be as quiet as possible. But Jimmy knew and he made me put my head on his chest and he stroked my red hair, which I had just cut short.

It's just that my heart ached so much. We had been in these tunnels so many times before, but this was different. It was really happening. It seemed so much darker now. Everything that we were doing now seemed so impossible and frightening. I felt buried alive. I know Jimmy and Kaz must have been feeling the same.

We left our families without a word. Without telling them where we were going. My God, I thought, what did we do? I wanted to go back. I was so afraid. Maybe there was still time to go back and start again. How easily afraid we become. Why always such a struggle to be strong? Why?

No, we closed that door behind us, but I could never really accept that. I tried to think of us as already dead, and there was nothing to be done about it. Why was I so afraid of death when it would have so much meaning when it came? It was easier that way. It was somehow comforting. It made what we did a little easier. There was nothing more to do, only to finish what we were down there to finish. Somehow it made me feel better, knowing that we were never coming back.

It was good that we kept busy. It was so important that we focus down here.

We had only been underground for a few days when we got up enough courage to try our first hit. I don't know how we decided on it. Maybe Kaz and Jimmy thought it was an easy target. I don't remember.

The first building we tried to bring down was in the financial district, on 23d. Strictly a test. It was early morning and Kaz planted the homemade bomb under the communication wires in the cable room. The bomb, made with sulfuric acid and glycerin, didn't explode, so we had to detonate it with a gunshot. We tried for a long time. I don't know how many bullets we used. It was pathetic. We couldn't hit a damn thing. Finally it flared and singed the cables but didn't take them out. We left in a hurry because the shots finally alerted a security guard. The guard didn't follow us for long. It must have been scary looking into those dark tunnels. No way he was going to do that on his pay.

Kaz was too close and burned his arm. Not a big deal. We had some medical supplies in the tunnels, like I said. Kaz had a fever that night at the apartment but it was nothing serious. But there was something about it, the amateurish attempt, Kaz's injury. You know that feeling you get, when you know you're in way over your head. I cried that night again and Jimmy held me. We tried not to let Kaz see. He was asleep anyway. I don't think he heard us.

The following day Jimmy asked me if I wanted out. I felt ashamed. That was it. No more crying. I would be brave. But I saw Jimmy wasn't sure about me. Looking back, I think it was the night that Jimmy decided what he would do when the time came. I think that was the night everything changed for him. I never saw it coming. I don't think you can really believe it until it happens.

It's not always the big things that cause the biggest changes in people. Sometimes it can be little things, like a look that was supposed to be hidden, that no one was supposed to see. Jimmy knew. I could tell. He saw something when he looked at me that time, and it made up his mind for him.

We learned from this failure. Two days later, after we were sure that the building's security people and electricians believed it was an electrical problem, Kaz used a stew of chemicals jammed into an iron pipe and lit with a fuse. I think it was permanganate and aluminum and some other shit, I'm not really sure.

It was beautiful, the cables blowing apart in a yellow flash. The bank's alarms going off, our retreat into the tunnels, trying not to laugh with the excitement and flush of this first corporate kill. Some kill. Two days later the bank was up and running again. We learned that The System repairs itself quickly. It's like one of those animals that grows back a leg or an arm. No problem. No real harm done. No one hurt. Business as usual.

It was fun seeing all the firemen and police running around. They didn't have a clue. They sent some of their people into the tunnels, fanning out, but they looked as scared as anybody would down there. They could have landed on an alien planet. They soon turned back.

By then, we were showering at the Queens apartment. Besides the daylight, it's the other thing I really missed. The feeling of hot water on my skin.

We laughed. It was exciting. Jimmy hated it when we laughed at those times. People in our position can't afford to laugh. This was serious work. We had to treat it the same way. It was fear that made us laugh. We were all afraid. It was just weird to see it in Jimmy.

I had never seen it in him before. It made me realize for the first time that maybe we really were already dead. We were just taking our time to catch up to it.

It was always a little weird and awkward with the three of us. It had to be, right? Jimmy and I only went back to college. Kaz and Jimmy practically came out of the same womb. Friends since they were seven or eight. Kaz loved Jimmy. I mean it's not like they could read each other's minds, that sort of eerie thing. Sometimes they could almost hate each other, not talk to each other, but it was like what they had between them went back to the dinosaurs. Something ancient and scary. It was that close a thing. I could never touch it.

It's not like Kaz was jealous of me and Jimmy, that he really hated me for it. That would have been normal. No, Kaz became my friend. He trusted me. He didn't trust anyone, not even some of his family. Only Jimmy at first. But he trusted me, and I started to trust him again. That's all we needed for what we were doing. We would need that trust later. And when it wasn't there, this helped destroy us.

Despite the lack of real success, we actually went to our next project feeling like we were legitimate. Kaz had learned from one of the maps about an abandoned elevator shaft that gave access to a narrow tunnel that got close to the computer rooms of an investment company. One afternoon we did a trial run. Jimmy and Kaz were able to climb down a rope ladder about twenty feet towards the bottom of the shaft. The shaft led to a narrow tunnel. Jimmy went first and they got about thirty feet into the tunnel when Kaz panicked and they backed out again. Kaz was breathing hard and he was really pale and scared, a wild look in his eyes. Claustrophobia. The experience from the past few days had changed him like that. Kaz became quieter. It was getting harder to reach him.

Then he said he wouldn't go back in the tunnel. Jimmy said he would go in instead. I didn't like it when he did these things. I was getting nervous again. We weren't even sure how close we were to the computer rooms. Using their flashlights, they could see that the tunnel just ended with a concrete wall. Kaz said he thought we were maybe a few feet from the rooms, or maybe twenty. He couldn't be sure. How could he? There was no real way of knowing unless you had the blueprints, which we didn't.

We tried to guess by going to the surface and looking around, but it was hard to imagine where the computer room was located. What made it worse, was that there was somebody looking at us from one of the other buildings. I'm sure he was looking at us. I panicked. We got out of there. He didn't look like a cop. More like a government type, in a gray suit. I don't know why I thought that, but he just didn't seem like a cop. Sometimes you have a sense about these things. He looked so small and he just stood there at one of the windows and watched us. Didn't even bother to move away. I know he was watching us. When we left he didn't follow us.

No, it was no good. Something was weird about that building. We backed off it. We kept looking around the city.

There was nothing in the papers or on TV about the killings in Long Island. That was really odd, but we didn't dwell on it and we didn't look any more. We wanted to forget about it, like it never happened. Maybe I wished it away, into the blind spot.

We should have known that something was up, even then. We should have known that these things don't happen without a reason, without The System wanting them to happen that way. Instead we ignored them and kept moving forward to what was waiting for us.

A few days later, we were in the lobby of the building of the insurance company that refused to provide medical treatment for Kaz's dad. We walked into the reception area, took a look around. A security guard stopped us, asked us what we were doing there. We gave him some cock and bull about being in the wrong building. He was so serious. Big man. Big protector of the status quo. Bought and paid for at nine dollars an hour. He asked us to leave. We were undesirables. The System had spoken.

So we left. Slow and easy. No disguises, we let him get a good look at our faces, who we were. We didn't really care if we were caught right there or six months down the road. Whatever happened, happened. It's when you start getting all worried about your safety and getting caught that The System finds you. It smells you. Because your fear makes you look for a method, a way to better your chances of survival. In a way you make a system, you become a system. That's when The System starts to understand you. That's what it expects. That's what it feeds on. That's how they find you and figure you out: they wait for you.

Two days later we blew up the insurance company's underground communications grid. Then we went above ground and entered the lobby and watched as everyone stood around wondering what to do. They were on company time after all and you could tell some even felt guilty they weren't working for a crummy half hour. Pathetic. The System really had those types. People who would do anything for it, always worried about what it thought of them, how they were doing. God forbid The System didn't like them. They would shrivel up and die. Those people were the worst, they were capable of doing anything The System wanted them to do – to catch us, or worse. They were The System's real soldiers.

The fire trucks showed up again. We heard some people say that the blast shook the building. That was something. It made us feel good. It made us feel more professional. Look, we shook a building! Crazy.

Our being there was stupid of course. We went to admire our work, to see the results. It was an ego thing and it almost got us caught. The firemen and the police hustled us out of the building with the others. That same security guard was there and he saw us leaving and you could see him slowly putting it together. Next thing he was walking towards us and calling his buddies on his walkie-talkie, like he was on the front lines in Kabul. You could see it in his eyes. Nobody fucks with The System, not on his watch.

We ran a few blocks. We could hear the security guard behind us telling us to stop. Then we entered a subway station and made our way back to our base. Nobody followed us. It wasn't his problem anymore. Let the subway handle it. Had there been more police when we were at the building, we would have been caught. Dumb. The System has people working for it at all levels. This was a reminder not to push it too much.

That's the last time we did that. After that we did our thing and that was that. We didn't bother to hang around with popcorn and watch the show.

The security guard would be describing us by now. They would be looking at CCTV. Maybe he thought there was a promotion in it. Maybe they would bump him up to ten an hour. Drone. Big protector of the status quo. Now they knew what we looked like. We would be all over the news. The theory would be tested now. Would they see us?

We didn't give a fuck. That night we bought tickets in New York and went to some theater off Times Square to see *Les Misérables*. I don't know how long it had been since any of us saw a play, maybe since high school. We were laughing all the way through it, we couldn't help it, it seemed so strange, these people play-acting at revolution and being brave. So they told us to leave.

They stared straight at us. Everyone did. No one recognized us, no one cared. There's something funny about people in a revolution going around singing. Revolution as entertainment. People always want to see others get killed doing what they want to do, what they should be doing. They would shake their heads, maybe have a little cry, then business as usual. We wondered if there would be people out there who would soon be thinking the same about us.

On the way back we walked into Times Square. There was a tall building there. An office building. Kaz stared at it a long time. We tried to get into the lobby but it was closed and we could see security everywhere inside. We asked Kaz why he was so interested in this building but he wouldn't answer us. Jimmy and I could sense trouble coming.

Next day we had to look at the newspapers. We poked our heads out from the apartment in Queens like gophers. There was nothing in the papers, nothing on TV. None of our faces were out there. What was going on?

There it was, buried on one of the back pages of the papers, something about a cable fire at the insurance company. Damn cable fire again. They must have thought all these cables were self-combusting or something. Everything was already back up and running. Surprise. We might have just as well kicked over some trash cans at a fire station and run away.

We weren't mentioned, there were no sketches of us. No description. Nothing. What was going on? We stayed at the apartment to get a good night's sleep. We talked about it.

Jimmy had worked as a security guard once, right after college. He said that deep down, despite all the macho bluster, most guards couldn't give a fuck about The System they were protecting. Most wanted to see it burn, just like us. They were just caught in its web, like everyone else, being sucked dry by corporate spiders. You don't even know you're caught until you try and escape. They want you to get married, have a family, get a mortgage. They call it responsibility, when really it's just a way of breaking you down, piece by piece, making you more vulnerable, submissive. They don't want you to think, to act. Only to keep moving in the same direction, with everyone else, keep those feet shuffling and don't ask any questions.

They want you to need them.

Maybe that was true about us too. Maybe we still needed them and just didn't want to admit it. Maybe we couldn't stand The System not noticing us. We had to change that. That was what we were thinking. Another ego thing. But it really wasn't necessary. We were to learn fast enough that The System needed us just as much. It would be important for them to keep us around as long as possible. We didn't know at that point just how much of a web was growing around us. We didn't know that we were just like all the others out there.

If we could just break up some of that web, who knows where it could go. Jimmy always kept us focused on that one thing, breaking up as much of that system's web as we could. That's all we could hope for. Anything else would be great, a real miracle.

Whenever Kaz or I would talk about what some anarchists had done, he would stop us. Screw Bakunin and Kropotkin and all of them. They could only complicate things. It could only make us freeze. We had to keep moving to that end that we had agreed on and that was waiting for us. It could only be us. If we stopped to think about what we were doing, it would all seem ridiculous and hopeless. I don't think we could move then.

I could see more and more how it all becomes instinct and sense. It has to be that way. Anything else would never stand up to the reality of what we were doing. You start looking in other places, at what other revolutionaries have done, you start looking for help there, you're lost. It'll pull you all over the place.

It hadn't always been the case with Jimmy. He'd changed a lot. In high school he was easygoing, shy. Wasn't political – a real bookworm, always reading history and philosophy. It was a little weird to see Jimmy burn those books, just like that. Kaz and Jimmy went back to grade school. They loved each other. Kaz had gone to an engineering school. Real techie type. Straight, right? When Kaz and Jimmy got back together after college, Jimmy couldn't believe how radical Kaz had become. They had read the same books – philosophy, politics – by some sort of osmosis, during all the time they were apart. Once they got over the initial awkwardness of seeing each other again, they were talking about their hatred of The System. Before you knew it, they were making these big plans on how to take a little bit of it down. And then I showed up. I was always complicating things, even when I was a kid. That's just the way it was.

We all moved on instinct and feeling in those early days. That's what I think Jimmy was trying to bring back again with us. He was more comfortable with that. Once you stopped to think about what was happening around you, that's when they have you in their freeze frame. That's when you're playing their game. You won't last long. They'll be waiting for you.

Kaz really opened up when he found out how I felt about The System. What it did to our families, how it was fucking as many people out there as it could. How I wanted to burn it down, start again. When he saw how serious I was, he began to trust me. A few days later I got the job at the hotel and we were scamming as many rich people as we could at the hotel and the clubs. Jimmy and Kaz surprised me that night in Queens with their plan.

At first I couldn't believe it, I thought they were joking. But Jimmy saw something in me that told him I would be interested. He just knew. Don't get me wrong. None of us wanted to die. It was no death wish. We just knew that if we could do even a small part of all we wanted to do, death would be a sure thing. It's like everything in life has a price, right? Death was our price. A little steeper maybe than most of the other prices. But we sure as hell weren't going to make it easy for them.

I was angry at Jimmy at first. Not because of the plan and the death part, but because they told me after, because they weren't sure about me. And they were right. I wasn't sure. I left the coffee shop that night and told them both to go and fuck themselves.

Was it because I was a woman, and maybe wanted to have kids and a backyard and everything that went with that whole you-know-what? Did I have to remind them that history is all about women giving it all up for what they believe in? Did I have to remind myself?

Jimmy came after me. Told me he was sorry. Told me to think about it. If I wanted to we could try going through the local political groups, the anarchists, the socialists, any of those groups. Any of those systems. I just had to name one of them and we'd join. And then what? We could fall in line, fall into the hierarchy, fall into The System, and most likely wind up doing nothing. This system feeds on everything around it, ingests it, makes it part of itself, like in that movie about the blob. Why not us?

My words, not Jimmy's. I know Jimmy would have done that for me. Not for Kaz. For me. For love. That was all I needed to hear. That he would do that. Then I was ready. That night we made the big plan. The suicide pact. We would make war on The System.

Looking back, though, I could see how Jimmy was already trying to talk me out of it. I didn't know it at the time. I don't even know if Jimmy did. I think that's why I did the opposite. Somehow all this was tied to my love for Jimmy. The more I thought he doubted me, the more I wanted to prove to him he was wrong. I don't know if he was testing my love for him.

Maybe. Maybe he just wanted me to give him a way out. Instead, I pushed him back into all this, and followed. All this time I was thinking it was Jimmy who drove all this. I found out later it was really Kaz. To him there was no compromise. The two of us created our own webs for different reasons, and we made sure Jimmy was caught in them.

Now that I have time to think about it, I know that's what it was. It was the fucking thinking. Always a problem, thinking. Thinking just made it messy. Jimmy was right about that. Once you stopped to think, it was over. You fall into the usual patterns. Your moves change, become predictable. Soon you're on The System's radar. Soon you're lost. It was just a matter of time. There was never an easy way with thinking, just more complications.

The weird part is, we began to feel more confident. And now that it was a cause, we became more understanding. Most people who worked in The System couldn't be blamed. The System controlled their minds and actions. Most were innocent. Sleepwalking, Kaz called it. Only when you woke them up all they wanted to do was go back to sleep. And they were angry that you disturbed them.

We looked at Federal Plaza. The FBI offices are on the 23rd floor. We argued about it then decided it was too risky.

We looked at it for days. It was weird. The building was like an ugly steel bunker above ground, in the city. Below, in the tunnels, it was something else: wide open, doors everywhere, no security that we could see, no cameras. We got enough courage to open one of the metal doors. There was nothing inside, just a small empty room. It was so quiet we couldn't hear anything, no machines or computers of any kind above us, in the building. It seemed too easy.

We watched some more. Nothing was going on down there. It was like the building was also watching us, waiting. We just had that bad feeling. We talked about it. Kaz said there weren't enough explosives to bring it down, and even if there had been, hundreds of people might be killed, even on a weekend. People who had nothing to do with the government or with corporations. No, it wasn't going to work. We decided to leave it alone.

We didn't even get into the lobby of the building. The whole place was jammed with long lines of people waiting to get into Immigration offices and get green cards. The last thing we wanted to do was blow up some innocent people trying to join The System and walk the line. If they wanted to become sleepwalkers like all the others, it was none of our business. That wasn't who we were after.

Just as we were about to leave, two men came out of the building and started walking along the line of people waiting to get in. One of the men was really odd-looking, a little bald guy wearing a gray suit that looked too big for him. It was hard to take your eyes off him. He was an odd-looking creature. They came along the line walking right at us. We were going to run but Jimmy told us to be cool and just stand there, like we were in line. They were talking to everyone in the line, working their way one by one, showing each person something, talking a few seconds with them, then the person would shake his or her head and the two men would move to the next one.

It was all I could do not to leave the line and walk away, maybe even run away. Jimmy held my hand and we waited. The warmth of his skin calmed me a little. When they got to us the little man in the gray suit showed us a piece of paper, a copy of a photograph of a young woman. The photograph had been digitally aged to give an idea of what she might look like today. At the top of the page in large black letters were the words: "Wanted For Domestic Terrorism." My heart stopped. I could see how much the woman in the photograph looked like me. Jimmy said he was sorry, Kaz and I shook our heads and the two men moved on. I stole a quick look at the man in the gray suit and his gray eyes scanned my face for a moment before he looked away. He didn't recognize me. There was no way he could know me. It didn't matter. I was scared shitless. We stayed in line another half hour until the men were finished and went back inside the building. It seemed endless. When they were gone we left the line and didn't look back. The whole thing had shaken us. We had seen that man before, the one in the gray suit. He was the one staring at us through the window from the building the other day. I was sure it was the same man. Jimmy and Kaz were not as convinced. It didn't matter. We had to be more careful from then on.

No, the building was bad luck. We left it alone. I don't know, looking back, maybe if we had tried, things might have turned out a little different. Who knows.

We were getting more frustrated. It was like a talent show for bomb targets. We were running out of contestants.

So what did we do? We decided to do the most fucking illogical thing we could: go back again to the insurance company building. We felt that we had let Kaz and his family down with that one. We wanted to do something more about it. This time we would get their attention. We decided to go back again, run right towards the lion. It was a mistake.

The thing was, there was no security there. Who in their right mind would come again to hit that same building? We snuck into one of the ventilation units which led up to a tiny room right above the air conditioning room. That room would be right next to the company's computer room. We were able to remove some of the panels in the ceiling and, using a rope, we lowered a shitload of explosives right beside one of the big air conditioners. We got out of there and tried to blow it, but nothing happened. Kaz was using a transmitter that he had built from his cellphone and it somehow jammed a circuit on the explosives. They just didn't go off. Kaz kept trying to get closer, crawling into the vent until he was almost in the room again, above the explosives.

We wouldn't let Kaz go any further. Kaz and Jimmy almost got into a fight about it. It was the first time I saw just how weirdly focused Kaz was when it came to his toys, and how dangerous he was at those times.

We talked about it. We let it go and left the explosives. I told them again I couldn't give a fuck about the insurance company. Not really. We should move on. Kaz thought it was being underground and the tunnels and all the interference with the metal. Remote control wouldn't work, not down here under this part of the city, in these tunnels. We almost got fucked by technology. Kaz couldn't keep away from his little gadgets.

We would have to do it another way. Trouble was either security or HVAC guys at the company would find the explosives, the police would come and they would send people into the tunnels and we would have done nothing so far. We'd be fucked. We decided that we needed to retrieve the explosives. Jimmy and Kaz argued about it again and I got mad and said I would go down. I had to prove myself. I felt like I had done nothing so far.

I could see Jimmy didn't want me to go, but he saw how important it was to me. We were revolutionaries, right? It was always dangerous. Kaz said it could be unpredictable. He was afraid that with so much electrical shit bouncing around down here, and us not knowing how things worked, it could be set off at any moment.

They were all for leaving the explosives. But I knew that if we did that it would be a day or two before they were found and we were hunted. It would have all been for nothing. Besides, we could use the explosives again. I went back in.

I'm no hero and I was fucking scared. Kaz and Jimmy lowered me into the room. I'm no heavyweight but they still had to lie flat and spread out and brace themselves with their legs against the walls so we didn't all fall in. That would have been the end of it.

I removed the trigger, and put the explosives in a plastic bag. Then I put pieces of the ceiling Styrofoam that had fallen into another bag and they got me up again. We patched the hole as best as we could and hoped it wouldn't be discovered too soon. I don't know if it was, and if it was I don't know what the company made of it.

All I know is that when we got out of there, we were drenched in sweat and too embarrassed to look at each other. Jimmy wouldn't talk to me for the rest of the day, and then we had a big argument. Reckless, that's what he called it, can you believe it? What did he think what we were doing was?

What we were doing wasn't safe. At all. It was reckless. That was the whole point. That's what we had talked about. He was the one always talking about being too soft, that we couldn't hesitate about what we were doing, and here he was, treating me like I was some kind of delicate child.

That's when it started to change, when we started to slip into The System, without even knowing it. Why didn't we just get the little car and the house in the suburbs and be done with it?

No, we knew we had to try for something bigger. Something that would finally get their attention. No hesitation. We had to prove to ourselves that we were different from what our fear told us.

I told you about the underground entrance to the building that Kaz had found on one of his explorations, the old ventilation shaft that led to the board room. And what would we do if and when we got there? Scare the shit out of them again when they were meeting? It was tempting. We could have used a little fun.

We looked at the maps again. We had found a way into the Museum of Art on Fifth Avenue. Take some art? No, what was happening to us? Our thinking was more bourgeois than what we were fighting.

The Chinese restaurant? You have to be kidding.

Why would we target them? They were just trying to use The System like everyone else. There had to be other targets that we could get to, targets with meaning for what we were trying to do.

We spent a day in the tunnels, looking for access points. We were frustrated. How hard could it be?

There were certain places that we agreed to leave alone. We didn't look at cultural icons like the MET or the MoMA. We could have. Kaz found a little HVAC shaft with computer wires that was more open than the others, right under the museum. Kaz had a whole list of weird out-of-the-way access points to places under the city, places urban explorer types didn't know anything about. He and Jimmy spent weeks looking around down there on their own, making their own maps. These art museums are paranoid about climate control and their HVAC systems and computers are amazing. But we left them alone. They were a harmless part of The System, a little opiate for the people. I told Jimmy and Kaz that I wouldn't go for any religious buildings. There was something there from my past, I couldn't do it. We left schools alone, although we joked about going back to Brooklyn to settle some old scores with our high school.

No, we were going for things that propped up The System, helped make it what it was. You know what I'm talking about. Corporations. We hated them. We vowed we would take as many down as we could before we were stopped.

Funny, I think at that time we were ready to stop. We had had enough. It's just that none of us wanted to be the one to say it, to admit we were failures. By the time these next things happened, it was too late. Everything just took on a life of its own. When we finally tried to stop it, it was too late.

Later that day we got drunk and decided that maybe the conference room in that bank wasn't such a bad idea after all. We needed to have some fun. We sensed it was over, but we just hadn't admitted it yet.

It wasn't fun. We worked our way into the HVAC system again and Kaz got stuck in one of the narrower ducts. It took us a few bottles of olive oil and two hours to get him out. Kaz almost dislocated his shoulder and freaked out from claustrophobia. Smelling of olive oil and with his torn clothes he looked like some weird salad. I don't know how we didn't get caught. But some of the time he was in there he was listening to a meeting in the board room.

Kaz said that they would stop talking and listen; they must have wondered what all the sounds were about, where the sounds were coming from. At one point Kaz and Jimmy started moaning again, like ghosts. They were laughing like idiots. I think it was one of the only times in all those weeks when we had some fun and laughed.

The people left the board room, probably to tell security about it. Despite what he went through, Kaz came out of the duct excited. While he was in there a weird thing happened. He remembered something. A building in Manhattan, a strange building near the Port Authority on 8th Avenue. He believed it was run by the government and some corporations that were storing enormous amounts of data on everybody.

It was strange. Kaz told us that only a few people know about his theory about this building. He had read about it somewhere. In this building were supercomputers that controlled most of the communications on the East Coast. He called it "the nexus point". The building was disguised, anonymous-looking, made to look like something else than what it was.

In reality, it connected to the government, which used it to gather information on everybody using social media. It recorded all conversations, analyzed chats, text messages, you name it, all with hidden codes and software that were almost impossible to detect. Rumor had it that a government worker was about to come out and blow the whistle on it but was killed on a New York subway train.

Kaz had come across this building when he was exploring the tunnels a few months earlier. It was one of the places we looked at. We didn't think about it much at the time, it looked like any other corporate building we were scouting. But then Kaz remembered that story about how there was supposed to be this harmless-looking building somewhere in Manhattan, set up to look like a bank or some other kind of business. Nothing unusual about it, except that it was actually a façade for this sinister operation used to control people. Why not?

Problem was, it wasn't the first building he thought was the nexus. At first he thought it was another building near Port Authority. That building was owned by Google. We couldn't find anything in the tunnels under the building. There was nothing strange down there. We went inside the building, into the lobby, and were stopped by security right away. It looked like any other office building inside, with people running around, looking uptight and serious. Turns out it was the old Commerce building. Lots of press about it, nothing too sinister. Google was developing some new version of its software.

Hell, you could even take tours there if you wanted. Couldn't be more open about it. Maybe that's what they wanted you to think all along, but it was out of our league anyway. Once you got into the tunnels underneath the building, it got real serious. Tighter than a bank vault.

Then there was the New York Times Tower at 1475 Broadway, in Times Square, that same building that caught Kaz's eye after we went to see *Les Misérables*. He was convinced the top two stories housed the supercomputers and programmers that were pumping out this government software that was going to control everyone. This time we wouldn't even go under to take a look at what was underneath it, and we didn't bother going into the lobby. What was the point? It would always be the same bullshit. Security guards in uniform, checking our bags, our IDs. It wasn't worth the hassle and the risk unless we were sure about it.

It was crazy, and we didn't take it seriously as we were half-worried about Kaz's sanity by then, but we were having fun. Looking back, we did have fun in those first days. Maybe we were too stupid to be afraid. Sometimes that's not such a bad thing.

When Kaz was stuck in that ventilation shaft it suddenly came to him. It was that other building, on 8th. It didn't bother him at the time, but now that he thought about it, there was something odd about the way the building was shaped underground, unlike any of the others. Like it was disguised somehow. He couldn't be sure, it was just a feeling.

Later we went under 8th Avenue and had a look. There was still nothing there, just tunnels and the usual storage areas. We walked into the lobby and tried to take the elevators but were again stopped right away by security. Jimmy and I were ready to sign in with some bullshit names and IDs, when Kaz said it was OK and told us we had made a mistake and had the wrong building. The security guy looked at us funny. I think he was ready to make a call when we left.

When we got outside we walked fast, and ducked into a coffee shop. Kaz had this intuition, you see, that it wasn't the right building. We almost got made and fucked because he had this intuition at first that it was the right building, this mysterious company that wanted to control everything. Now his intuition told him that it wasn't the right building. Fuck. That was the last time we believed Kaz about anything. It wasn't fun anymore.

What was it going to be? We were into intuitions now. What was happening? Were we going to bring in the Ouija boards? We had a loud argument in that coffee shop. It had been a long time coming. We let it all out. Kaz didn't trust me, he didn't trust the way I showed up suddenly in Queens that day six months ago. I told Kaz that I didn't think he believed in what we were doing, that I thought he just wanted to play with his toys, it was just another game to him. It hurt me that he didn't trust me. I don't know if it hurt him that I didn't trust him, I couldn't give a fuck, but truth is I did, I trusted Kaz and I wanted him to trust me. It's always been like that with me. Why couldn't others see? Why couldn't they see what I saw? I could make them see. It was right there. Just look. I could help them look. All they had to do was be willing to believe. Then they would see.

It was the same with Kaz. He didn't know that I loved him, almost as much as I loved Jimmy. I was just always afraid that Kaz didn't love me. I never knew until the end how wrong I was, how it was I who didn't see. How hard Kaz was trying to make me see.

I knew it was all about Jimmy, that Kaz loved him, that we were doing everything to avoid talking about it. That Kaz and I, despite Jimmy, we loved each other too. And we should have talked about it, but we never came around to it. We went at each other like enemies. Until Jimmy had enough and said he was sick of it and how sad it made him. And I hated Jimmy for that, because he didn't come down on Kaz. He didn't support me. And we let it simmer after that, and it was a mistake. I think that's why Kaz didn't break it off completely with Vecchio. One mistake makes another and so on, until there's nothing left that you can rely on. We never ended it there and then and that was a mistake. We should have ended it then. Left the tunnels. Moved to fucking Indiana. Why not? We still had a chance, I believe we did, but sometimes there are other things that move you along, for whatever reason. You know what I mean? It was never just the three of us. There was always something there, moving us around, like pieces on a board. We were never really alone. I always felt that there was more than just the three of us. And I came to hate that other thing that was with us, that thing that seemed to hate us, and wanted nothing more than to destroy us.

No, Kaz wasn't finished with his intuitions yet. More black magic. So we went back to take another look in the tunnels that afternoon. For the next few days we looked in those tunnels for something that probably didn't exist. The big hit, the one that would make it all worthwhile. That's what we were looking for.

We split up. Always a mistake. It was breaking one of our most important rules. Then it happened. Later that night, on the night of the third day of looking, Kaz came back to us and said he had found it. Yeah, sure. We didn't believe him, but it didn't matter. That other thing that I mentioned, the thing that was always with us, wouldn't let us stop.

That same night we went down and looked. I had to admit something was up. The building that Kaz believed in was off on one of the side tunnels and it was easy to miss. It didn't look like any other part of the subway tunnels. It was about twenty feet across, all old concrete, all solid, no windows or access points. When we put our hands up to the concrete we could feel that it was cold. You couldn't hear anything inside, it was quiet. We didn't know what to think. There were no elevator shafts that we knew of that came this far down into the tunnels. It was too quiet for HVAC, unless the walls were so thick that we couldn't hear anything anyway.

A ten-story building. The bottom floor under the city was all wrong. It was like a separate part of the building above, built to one side; in case the building collapsed, it would miss all the communications beneath. OK, it looked weird but that didn't mean a thing. There are lots of weird buildings in New York.

When we went to the surface we found where we thought the concrete block should be. It was the bank we had visited a few months ago, real traditional-looking, granite, nothing special. To Kaz this was it. It was right in front of us. Maybe. But this time we weren't going to leave it to premonition and a Ouija board.

We went to a library and researched. We got easy passes into the city archives and looked through microfilm and found an old document from 1912 that talked about details for building a large private elevator shaft for a wealthy prick in those days. There was a drawing of the building from the same time. It was the same building that was now a bank. It got better.

One of the documents showed an elevator shaft door installed at the bottom. The owner, a banker named Stewart, had instructed the builders of the elevator shaft to extend it underground, into the subway tunnels that had just been built and started operating. Who knows for what reason, it didn't say. Maybe the guy thought it was the end of the world and he wanted an escape hatch into the tunnels under the city, just in case. Maybe he was a crook and had enemies. Those kinds of crazies have been around for a long time. They're all over the city, maybe even more of them today than before.

We made a copy of everything then went back down. Where the door was supposed to be, the concrete was a little different, like it had been added later. Anybody could see it.

We found the article where Kaz had read about the nexus building. In a local radical newspaper. It wasn't hard to locate the reporter.

He was living in an old walkup in Soho. When he saw us he was scared. He thought we were from the government. We talked to him and it was a waste of time. You couldn't have been any vaguer about details.

I was against it from the start. We couldn't trust the reporter, or anyone else.

It was a bad idea. The man was a crackpot. Here we were talking with conspiracy peddlers and looking at hunches. There was no end to it.

The prick wanted to gain from his information. From something that he should be proud to bring down. He wanted us to pay him. Great. Even the crazies in The System are kneejerk capitalists who want to fuck you. There was no escape. I was starting to get violent thoughts about this guy. The asshole tried to snap a photo of us with his digital camera as we were leaving. That did it.

We took the camera away from him and Kaz smashed it on the floor. The prick would have shown the photos to the cops to try and get money. Jimmy hit him, so did I. We all hit him. He fell to the floor. He was making a lot of noise, like some weird animal. He wouldn't stop so I pulled my gun out and pointed it at him and told him to be quiet, but he didn't listen. Jimmy hit him again and he stopped making noise. Something was seriously wrong with this guy.

I still had the gun pointed at him. My hands weren't shaking. I was surprised and proud of that fact. It was anger that kept me steady. It was always like that with me. When I got angry I would go into this cold focus. I was so focused, so how come I couldn't remember that when I really needed it?

We left him. He knew nothing. It was the same thing as the article. About a certain company that was a kind of hub for all the communications of all companies on the East Coast. No, it wasn't Google or Facebook or any of those other bullshit cool companies that were only out there to fuck the sleepwalkers. It was some mysterious software company, something hush-hush, something that the government was involved in. It was disguised as a bank, a modern building like any other office building, like any other bank, on Lexington Avenue.

The reporter said that if the communications at this building were taken out it could shut down the city, maybe the entire Northeast, like that time with the power failure in the '60s, only bigger. Nobody knew what the building really was about, so the security was pretty abysmal. That's what he said. I didn't believe him. How do you believe someone who makes sounds like an animal?

We knew that he would phone the police about us and try and get money from them. At the very least he would be describing us.

That night we argued again. We did that more and more now. Now we were listening to crackpots and having more premonitions. This time even Jimmy had enough. I never heard them argue like that before. If you didn't know any better you would think they were going at it because of philosophy, commitment, direction. It was nothing so noble. It was much older than that, something very simple. I knew it was about me. We were after the same thing, Kaz and I, something we couldn't share anymore, but something neither of us was about to give up. Something that stood between Kaz and Jimmy.

What happened was Jimmy won. He always did with Kaz. We went back to doing what we had done before. We got better at it. I think that was the time that it all changed again, when we felt that we could really do it, that it had a reason, a purpose. I don't think we were really convinced until then.

I had my anger and it made me stronger. I was still afraid. I would always be afraid, I wasn't like Jimmy, but I knew then that I could go through with it. See it through. Maybe we all could.

I would try and keep my anger simmering somewhere inside me, aware and ready. It was this idea that kept my fear away, at least for a time. It wouldn't be that difficult, I thought. There are always things to be angry about, right?

Then Jimmy said we should take another look at what Kaz was talking about. The nexus building. It was sudden, just like that night with the safe in the hotel. Here was another thing for me to be angry about. I realized it would never change, that it would keep going like this until we stopped or they killed us. Jimmy would never be as much a part of me as I was of him. I could never reach the part of Jimmy that Kaz had the key to. Never.

I didn't talk to Jimmy the rest of that day. He never knew what it was about. Even if I told him, he would never understand. I could never reach that part of him through words. And that was about all I had left. I knew Jimmy wouldn't listen to me now about leaving the tunnels, the city. It was too late for that.

I went along, waiting to see if something would change. We looked up information on the bank. It seemed legitimate enough, a small bank based in New York, no other branches, at least none that were listed. That was odd.

I thought Kaz was going too far with all this bullshit, until we went into the bank to take a look. Then I thought maybe there was something to it.

We walked into this place, and I tell you it looked like any other bank, with tellers and offices and a few people who looked like managers running around, looking all business, like at any other place. We went up to one of the tellers and opened an account. There was nothing weird about it, as far as I could see. It was just a bank. I won't tell you its name. It was nothing out of the ordinary, but Kaz said the computers and network systems were all below, out of sight, in the tunnels.

There was something else that was odd about the place. No elevators, at least not that we could see. No one from the outside came in to use the elevators to go to the higher levels. No one who was already in that building went up. Everyone stayed there, on ground level, looking busy. Watching.

Then we saw the cameras. Everywhere. A couple of security guards appeared from nowhere and stared at us. We asked them where the elevators were. They told us the elevators were not working. It would be some time before they were fixed. There were no elevator servicemen coming or going that we could see.

Not far from the door leading to the stairs was another security guard.

We got the message and left.

When we got outside again we looked up and saw all the windows in the building were the kind that you couldn't see through, tinted with something dark.

The next day we broke the rule again. We split up. And we had a big scare.

Jimmy went into the bank again. Kaz and I scouted the tunnels under the nexus building and found the communications cables. There were four enormous rooms with cables. Kaz made some sketches.

In that time we saw only one security guard. He came in, checked the rooms in a few seconds, wrote something on a sheet attached to a hanging clipboard then left. The strange part was that this security guard was carrying an automatic machine gun.

When the guard was gone, Kaz checked the clipboard. Security came around every three hours.

When we saw Jimmy again he said he had tried the stairs at the bank. He waited until the security guard left, then went through the door up the stairs. He made it to the fourth level. There were no doors before that, on any level, just blank walls. He tried the door at the fourth level but it was locked.

He could hear weird humming sounds on the other side of the door. Kaz said it had to be the main computer and switching rooms. Something sinister was going on. Jimmy went up to the fifth level, same thing. Door locked, humming on the other side. Same with the sixth level. And then the stairs just ended, dead end. No more doors, no more levels.

Yet from the outside the building looked like it had about ten stories, maybe more. It was hard to tell. It didn't make any sense. There was something going on there with the government, with corporations. It was no ordinary operation. Kaz had to be right.

We all went into the bank again. Jimmy wanted a closer look. There were people at the tellers just like before and some offices nearby, with only one manager in his office and a few customers waiting to talk with him. The other offices seemed empty, or at least their doors were closed. Jimmy went up the stairs again to get a closer look but was stopped by a security guard. He told Jimmy that it was a restricted area.

When Jimmy got back down to the main level again he saw the stairs ended just below. There was no door or stairs to the basement. More weird shit.

Then security guards took him. Jimmy signaled us not to do anything, to just sit tight. We were dumb. We wouldn't split up again after that, at least not until the end. Kaz and I left and waited outside.

They took Jimmy into a room and sat him down and waited. Jimmy said he was trying to get up to where the corporate offices were, that he had a complaint about his account. Thank God Jimmy had complained to one of the tellers in the lobby before he went up the stairs again. She had told him to wait near the office of one of the managers, but Jimmy only waited a minute before he saw the guard move and then he took the stairs.

At least he had a legitimate excuse. Jimmy said that after he told them this they sat there in silence for maybe fifteen minutes, then the door opened and this little guy in a suit came in and told the security guards to leave.

Jimmy played dumb. The guy in the suit confirmed his story about the teller, saw that Jimmy had an account at the bank, checked his ID. This guy was no banker. He was government. Jimmy was sure of it. The guy in the suit copied everything Jimmy had then let him go.

We were getting tense waiting for Jimmy. We all knew now it wasn't just a bank. It was something else and whatever it was, it was well protected.

When Jimmy came out again, we left in a hurry. They put a tail on us. We walked awhile then went into a restaurant and sat there for some time, long enough for the car following us to finally drive off.

In that car were two men. The one in the passenger seat was huge and bald. We didn't get a good look at the driver, who was smoking. They looked straight at us when they left. We made it back to the apartment without being followed, but we couldn't be sure.

I almost killed Jimmy when we got back. I was so angry with him. What was all this about staying together? What did we talk about? And now he was going off and making these sudden decisions on his own. I didn't talk to him for a long time. It made me realize that it was different when we weren't together. It made me realize how scared I was without him.

When Jimmy and I were together there wasn't anything I couldn't do. When I wasn't with him, this whole thing we were doing, it didn't make any sense. It just made me feel scared and frozen. I was angry because I knew then that my whole commitment to what we were doing was nothing if we weren't together. I felt hopeless and weak. Without Jimmy, I couldn't do it. And yet Jimmy looked fine without me. That pissed me off.

It didn't matter, the argument between Jimmy and me. What happened, happened. I knew then that I couldn't be like Jimmy, no plan, just see what happens. I realized I wasn't like that, I would never be like that.

I was afraid because I knew we were on The System's radar now. This was real. The System was coming to life. It was starting the hunt. Maybe the man in the suit who talked to Jimmy was the same guy I saw looking at us a few days ago from the window across the street. I wasn't sure. It sounded like him.

There was no doubt that something was fucked up about that building. Whatever it was, it was no bank. We talked about it. Maybe it was too easy. There was something too inviting about it. But it was too important to pass up. Even with that guy in the suit somewhere out there.

Things began to move fast after that.

We waited a few days and watched the building while we got ready. There were cars parked there. I was sure they were watching us. We didn't see the big bald guy or his partner and we didn't see the little guy in the suit. That made us nervous. Something told us this might be our last chance. We had to act quickly, no bullshit.

We would move the explosives in tomorrow, Friday, and blow it up the next day. Or maybe Sunday. We hoped that no one would be working inside. We talked about it. I found a payphone and called the main number at the bank to find out if anyone would be working in the new computer facility on Sunday. The woman on the other end asked me who I was. I didn't tell her. She told me to wait. After a few minutes she came back on and told me there were no new computer rooms. Yeah, sure.

She was keeping me on the line as long as she could. They were tracing it. I didn't care. I hung up and got away as fast as I could. We waited nearby for a time but no police showed up at the payphone.

It was always good to move explosives into the tunnels on busy weekdays. Saturdays are not bad, it's still busy in the city, but Sunday is quiet, the city is almost empty, and you'd be surprised how many police and people are in the city on Sundays, bored and moving around and watching. Just watching. Looking for trouble. It was too risky. So we moved the explosives a few days before.

We took different ways back to the apartment. We were always splitting up now. It was our new way. I hated it. We were becoming more paranoid about getting caught. The taste for survival was creeping into us, getting stronger. We didn't talk about it, but we knew. So much for winging it on instinct, so much for the suicide pact. We didn't talk it now. It only took a few weeks to start coming apart. I hated it.

Sometimes we would meet again somewhere near the apartment. Once, when we were a few blocks away, we thought there was a car following us. We split up again. I saw two men in the car, then the car left. We didn't see it again that night. We thought it was nothing. Every car now looked like it was coming after us, seemed to slow down and watch us. We were falling apart.

A day later they found the apartment in Queens. Something told us not to be there. We took photos of the police looking around, asking people questions. One of the same two detectives, the bald one, was there. The other, his partner, was in the car, smoking. He was the same one who was driving the other day. They seemed to be in charge of all this shit.

We got a good look at them now. These two were the ones on the hunt, the lead dogs The System had sent to find us. We studied the photos we took. I didn't like the look of the bald guy. He looked big and mean, you could hear him barking at the others, even from where we were. Impatient prick, the way he suddenly moved towards someone. Intimidating. Threatening. I was afraid of this one. Why couldn't he have been in the building we blew up a few days ago?

The other detective smoked. A lot. He was dark-haired and looked Hispanic and seemed calmer. There was something softer about his eyes. They looked sympathetic. I remember thinking at that moment, *if we are ever at the mercy of these two, my money is on the calm one.* With the other one, we would be dead.

These are the two looking for us, we thought. These are the two who will end it soon, one way or another.

At night the next day we went to the house we rented in Brooklyn. It was the first time we had been there in a while. We stayed in the park across the street, sitting on one of the benches, and we watched. We watched a long time. We were beginning to learn to be patient, that there was a time to watch and wait. Sometimes it was the most important thing you could do. It seemed OK. We didn't see anything weird, nobody sitting in cars nearby. It looked clear. So damn quiet. A nice neighborhood. That was Jimmy's idea again. Pick a nice quiet neighborhood, with big yards, lots of space between the houses. The kinds of people living in those houses never bothered one another, never bothered to know who was living right beside them. There was a lot of room to ignore one another, a lot of space to be anonymous, to believe everything was great. Just don't do something that would get their attention. Just like The System. Don't get on their radar.

No, it looked fine. I had never been patient. I was ready to cross the street and go in through the back door. I wanted a shower, hot water, and not the smelly stuff we tried to wash with in the pipe room in the tunnels. I wanted to open a refrigerator, eat food, sleep in a bed. I wanted to feel Jimmy beside me in that bed. I wanted to make love to him in that bed. Fuck this, I wanted to go in, just for one night.

But we waited. Even Kaz was ready to go in, but we waited. And then, just when Jimmy relented and said we could make our way across to the back of the house, we saw a light, just for a moment, through a window in one of the top rooms. It was only a moment, but it was everything. It scared us to death. We went back to the bench in the dark and waited. There was nothing else, no more lights, no cars, no one waiting in those cars, but it didn't matter. We saw them everywhere in the shadows now. Waiting for us. More patient than us. There was nothing left except the tunnels. Nowhere else to go. No more options.

We left the park and avoided the bus route that we had taken to come out. We walked a long time and took a different route back into the city, through the Bronx. It took forever, and when we reached the city we ate a late dinner and then we realized just how close we were to a familiar place and we took a chance and checked into the same boutique hotel we had worked at a year ago. It was Jimmy's idea. I don't know if we just didn't care or were too tired to argue.

No one recognized us. How fucking much we had changed in a year, I thought. We used fake IDs. We even stayed in the same suite Jimmy and Kaz almost got caught in, the one with that Norwegian safe. No one said or did a thing. I wouldn't be surprised if that tiny camera was still working above check-in. Good luck getting anything from our credit cards. We took hot showers and ordered room service. We got the best night's sleep we had had in months. I can't remember the last time I felt that safe. There, right in the middle of The System, right where the lion was sleeping.

Jimmy and I screwed as quietly as we could, with Kaz in the next room. I know he could hear us. I wanted him to. I hated him for loving Jimmy, for Jimmy loving him. Jimmy and I screwing, I felt like it was the only bit of power I had left, and I wanted Kaz to see it.

There was nothing conditional about it. It was Kaz who convinced Jimmy about all this, about what we were doing. I knew it was Kaz. I didn't want any more of it. I was done. Now was my chance. I thought I could convince Jimmy. With just the two of us alone. We talked. Jimmy was in a good place that night. He didn't want to talk. His eyes got hard. He got restless. And the more we talked the more distant we became with each other. I could see it in Jimmy's eyes. Betrayal. That's when I knew there was nothing unconditional about our love. It was tied in with everything else. With Kaz and the fucking system. As long as I loved what we were doing, Jimmy loved me. There was no possible love outside that.

I said there could be another way of doing this. We could work within The System, we could do it and there was still time. We had made a point, we had done some good things, gave them a scare. We could convince Kaz, Kaz would listen to you, I told Jimmy. You could convince him. We could be out of the city the next day. It was our decision. Now was the time. They were closing in. Please.

I saw Jimmy was testing me again. Testing my loyalty, my strength, my commitment. Especially my love. And I was testing him. He asked me again if I wanted to leave. I said not without him. I wanted to say that if he loved me he would leave with me, but I didn't. I sensed that if I did I would never see him again. That would be the end of it. I was afraid and I would later regret not asking it, because when I finally had the courage, it was too late.

We left the hotel without paying, and we stayed in the city. Another chance lost. There wouldn't be another one. I knew that. Jimmy and I barely talked for the rest of that day. Kaz looked at me like it was my fault that Jimmy was that way. Kaz and I were never the same after that. I was done with Kaz. I just went through the motions from then on. I was freewheeling it, just like Jimmy had wanted all along. Well he had it.

The nexus building became their obsession. I acted like I was on board again. Jimmy and I were like that. We could never stay red hot angry with each other. Not for long. It was I who always came around of course. A smile, then the embrace, the forgiveness. On the true path again, together. I always let Jimmy take the noble way back in. That was a mistake.

Soon I was excited myself about the nexus building. What the fuck was it? Could the stories be true? It all seemed so much more mysterious now than it did before. We were all excited, even Jimmy was convinced now. We had to do something, move towards something, anything. We were going around in circles.

The next day we went down to the tunnels to take another look. Kaz brought some tools with him and we started chipping away at the concrete. In a couple of hours we had cleared enough of it, about half a foot deep. It wasn't very good concrete; it was soft and easy to remove. There was the metal door. Around it was some odd material. We realized after chipping away more of the concrete that it was something called glazed terracotta. The same material mentioned in the old documents in the archives.

It didn't take long to clear the rest of the material and expose the door. There was an old Yale padlock on it and that was all. The door was rusty and flimsy. Could this be some forgotten part of the building from 1912, a separate section that the people in the bank above knew nothing about? No, impossible.

We didn't do anything else. We left and talked about it later. Suddenly Jimmy was anxious. Something wasn't right. It was Kaz and I who wanted to go behind the door, at least to find out what was on the other side. We could at least look. We had come this far. We had to know if this was it.

When we went down again Jimmy stood watch. He thought he saw something, someone moving, but it wasn't that strange down there. We were always seeing people, just for a moment, before they were gone again. We were so damn jumpy. It wasn't a good sign.

There was still no sound on the other side of the door. It only took a few minutes and we had the door off. No alarms or sirens. It was all dark.

We brought flashlights in. We were in the old narrow shaft. There was no elevator, no cables, only a spiral metal staircase that went right up to a concrete ceiling. The staircase was still solid. Kaz and I walked up as far as we could, to only a few feet from the ceiling. We could hear the sounds of machines. Kaz got excited.

"Air conditioning," he said, "server cooling racks, big ones. There are fucking big computers in there."

We didn't question Kaz about it. He was the engineer, the computer guy, right? If he said there were big cooling units up there with big computers, he would know. At that point we just wanted to blow it up.

It was perfect. This was it. This was our big one. This would be our last one. I got excited. I could have Jimmy back again. Kaz said he could bring in heavy enough explosives to bring down the floor and maybe everything above us. Maybe it wouldn't amount to much, but it would at least stop this operation for a little while, whatever it was. Maybe it would at least scare the shit out of them, maybe we could let the media know, maybe the media could find out more about it, maybe it would cause a scandal, maybe it would be all over the internet, at least until The System shut it down, maybe the government and these corporate social networking fucks would have to close it down and run, maybe it would get some of these other protesters organized and working together, maybe it would cause a revolution. Even a fucking small one. Yeah, right.

We didn't care. This one act would be our purpose, our mission, our reason for doing all of this. Whatever happened, it was worth it.

We thought that maybe we were just lucky, that it all fell into our laps. Why not? It had been Kaz's Holy Grail. Now it was ours.

From then on we moved forwards with purpose.

We brought in an air drill, a real quiet one. Kaz had bought it from one of the fences because he thought it was cool. It was expensive, but it was so quiet you could barely hear it. In an hour we were through the concrete floor. It was about six inches thick. Then we hit metal. Kaz said it wouldn't be a problem. We had enough explosives to blow everything up.

We came back a few times over the next few days to set up the explosives. Kaz secured them to the ceiling with a shitload of duct tape and this special kind of tape that could stick to anything, something that he had bought on the net. We could hear the machines above us, they were going all day and night. Kaz drilled a small hole through the metal in the ceiling then got one of these pinhole TV cameras, the kind on the thin wires, and tried to see into the room. It was too dark to really see anything clearly. We could make out some machines but I couldn't really tell what they were. Kaz got excited. He said the machines were supercomputers.

"IBM Power 575s," he said, "seven or eight of them. No way those are for a bank. You could run a country with those." Kaz said those computers had to use a system of copper pipes filled with water to cool down the processors. He said these computers use a lot less air conditioning and power than the older models.

"These things were developed at IBM's Zurich lab, I mean it actually starts with fairly hot 45 centigrade water, running it past the fucking hot microprocessors to bring them down to 85 centigrade operating temperature, which then heats the incoming water beyond 50 centigrade. I mean the water's hot enough to be used as waste heat for building warming or municipal use. I'm not kidding. That's why there aren't many ACs in there. They don't need them. This place is no fucking bank!"

Jimmy and I had no idea what Kaz was talking about. We asked him if we could blow it up, and he said hell yeah, let's do it.

We were going to do it the next day, Sunday. Nobody would be working there, at least we hoped the lady on the phone was telling the truth. We would at least try and make sure no security guards were in the room. We couldn't guarantee anything.

That afternoon and evening we got everything ready. There was no one in the tunnels. It was quiet. It was easy this time. Like everything had been cleared just for us.

After we agreed that night that this would be our last target, something happened to me. I was so happy. I wanted to live. Maybe we would live after all, maybe we could still get out of this, and our families and everyone else would never find out who we really were, what we did. Could we imagine that? It was like the sun came out again for me, just for a short time.

With that hope came a new fear. I was suddenly terrified of the tunnels, of the bombs, the guns, getting caught, everything. What was happening to me? None of this had any meaning for me. What were we trying to do? I wanted to go and hide somewhere, I wanted things to be quiet again. Then come out again, into the city, like I was reborn. Same with Jimmy, with all of us. Start again.

We would do it and get out. No one hurt, we didn't want to hurt anyone. I was so happy. This was it. Our big statement, our last one, and then we would be out, maybe go back into The System again and no one would know, no one would be any wiser.

Jimmy and I could do things together, maybe get married, and we would never talk about it with anyone else over the years, maybe only exchange the odd glance and smile. It might even be fun, a little scary but fun. Our big secret. We could even try and change things from the inside, a little at a time. It would be like penance, like service to the community. I was ready.

After all, what did The System have on us really? Some video camera shots of us. We could be anybody, none of us had any records, any photos that could be traced, any fingerprints. Nobody else knew what we were doing, Vecchio and the other fences included. Everything we had bought over the months was with cash or fake IDs. Nothing could be traced. No, we couldn't think of anything that could be traced. We could get out in time. It could work.

Funny how we had all changed by then.

Getting stuck in the tunnel did it to Kaz. He became paranoid about any kind of enclosed space after that. He couldn't last more than a few hours in the subway tunnels anymore. He had to go up for air every so often, into the city, like a seal. I don't think he was thinking straight. I could see Kaz was starting to panic more and more.

No, if we were going to do it, we had to do it fast. Jimmy and I didn't have the same skills as Kaz. We needed him to do this and get out. Fast.

All of us changed. I became scared of being around people. I was no longer looking for that blind spot. I avoided security cameras, public places. Screw all that illogical crap, I was terrified. Everyone seemed to be looking at me now. Everyone seemed to know about us, about what we were doing. My confidence was gone. It was happening to all of us. Once the confidence goes, we knew The System would close in quickly. We wanted to live again, and that was our big weakness. That's when it has you. And it definitely had us.

That night before Sunday was the longest. It never ended. We waited and our nerves got worse. If it hadn't been for Kaz and his need to do something to that building, I think Jimmy would have let it go, and we would have left right then, at that moment. I wouldn't have hesitated. God, we could have been free. Maybe we could have had a chance. But that damn building, it was too good for Jimmy and his pride to pass up. It was there, waiting for us. It represented everything that he hated, all in one little bundle. It represented a way to finally succeed, with one hit, to make up for all the other mistakes we had made.

The slate would be clean and our work would be done. What we had done in those weeks, it would have meant at least something. Then we could start again. If we had only left the day before… But maybe by then it didn't matter anymore. What we didn't know is that it was already too late.

We waited. That other thing that was always with us, that I know was trying to destroy us, made us wait there, unsure, frozen. Always waiting.

In the end we decided to go ahead with everything. It was that sudden. We would take the building down. In all that time I never said anything to Jimmy about how I really felt about him, about all this. Fool.

That morning Kaz wound up packing that room below the computers with a lot more explosives than he first put in. Maybe he wanted to make a statement after the previous failures. I don't know. None of us were thinking straight by then. It was just good to act, to do something.

Kaz hid the explosives timer and we went to the surface for a break and some air. By then I was getting anxiety attacks being down there. We ate in a restaurant across the street and a few blocks down. We sat there and waited. There was a car parked across the street with two men sitting in it. Undercover police? Maybe. They paid no attention to us. Maybe Jimmy's theory of hiding in plain sight really had something to it. Or maybe they were just dumb. Maybe they were always just dumb. Maybe it had nothing to do with us. We waited. The time was getting close.

Kaz got nervous all of a sudden and said he had to check on something. No, we wouldn't let him go. It was all of us or none. So we all went back down. Something told Kaz that not all was right. Another damn premonition. Sure enough when we reached the communications room with the cables there was the guard checking around. He wasn't supposed to come by for another hour.

Twenty minutes to go. We didn't know what to do. Then someone else came down the elevator. It was the little man in the suit that Jimmy had seen. It was the same man I had seen in the window. He started looking around with the guard. We didn't know what was happening. Did they know all about us? It would only be a matter of time before they found the explosives in the other room. We sat there frozen, just looking at each other. We thought we heard people coming along one of the tunnels towards us. We couldn't be sure.

We called it off. That was it. It had been decided for us. We were free. I was so fucking happy. Kaz removed the timer and we left and went back up to the street. The police car in front of the restaurant was gone. We walked a few blocks when we heard and felt the blast. After a second we realized it was another building nearby, not the bank.

At first we couldn't believe it. Jimmy and I thought our explosives went off by accident, maybe the cooling system with the computers set it off, maybe some vibrations, but Kaz said no, it was impossible. It must be an accident, a gas explosion, but we knew better. It was no coincidence.

When it went off, it was like an earthquake. There was a rumble then everything shook. The windows in the building shattered. Everything came apart. It was such a big explosion. No, it couldn't be ours.

We saw some people lying on the sidewalk outside the building. A little boy and his mother and an old woman, out for a walk in New York on a Sunday. They had all passed us a few seconds before on the street.

I wanted to run to them but Jimmy caught me and wouldn't let me go. I shook myself free and ran up. I didn't care. They were lying there. Glass everywhere. They had been crushed by it. The woman was still cradling her little son, trying to protect him. The old woman, probably the grandmother, was still alive. She stared at me but she had been cut pretty badly. She died right there. Within a few seconds.

There were people crying, some hurt. Some were standing around, some sitting. Others were sleepwalking, lurching around, like those people in the zombie movies, looking for answers. There was a fire in one of the rooms of the building, at street level, and someone was staring at it, not sure what to do. Nobody was trying to put it out.

Pretty soon we heard the fire trucks and police cars. I felt someone's arm. It was Jimmy. I didn't recognize him at first. I could have been anywhere, I was so dazed. I let him lead me away. He put his arm around me and we walked slowly, didn't look back.

We entered one of the office buildings. People were coming out to look. What were they doing there on a Sunday? They might have been looking at us, I don't know. Anything was possible now. Nobody stopped us. I kept my head down and we took the stairs to the basement parking level. I was numb. I could have gone anywhere at that moment, I wouldn't know where I was. We walked across the parking garage, opened a door and entered the subway. Kaz suddenly appeared and scared the hell out of me. I lost it. I started beating him. Jimmy tried to stop me but Kaz told him to let me continue. We could see that he was also in shock. I beat him until I was exhausted then they led me down to a maintenance area and eventually to one of our safe rooms. It all looked so strange to me now.

We sat there a long time. No one spoke. Kaz looked so white that I thought I had beaten the blood from his face. Then he began to cry. It was very soft, like internal crying. The kind that happens when you're really hurting.

What was happening to us? It was all coming out now. This was the end, seeing that boy and his mother. No, it was over.

It had all changed. Just like that. You could still smell the smoke from where we were. A little boy. His mother. His grandmother. The System would take notice now. It was aroused. Fully awake. They would be in the tunnels soon. All of them. The media would get involved. We had finally stirred it and it would come looking for us with a vengeance. Even if that wasn't our bomb. It didn't matter anymore. We had to get out.

We were underground again and it wouldn't take long for them to figure it out. And then they would be after our families. I couldn't think of that. I couldn't think of that kind of weakness and vulnerability, the pain our families would go through. It would freeze me completely.

We had enough of explosives, of the suicide pact, of everything. It was over. There was still money in the bank accounts. They wouldn't know about it. Not yet. We could try and get out. How would they know we had gone underground? We could get the money and leave the city. We would have maybe a day or two. It was at least something.

We never made it to the bank tellers. We waited outside the bank for a time, to see if it was clear. Then we saw there were police everywhere. We were followed through two office buildings before we found another utility door leading to the subway. They knew now that we were under the city, moving around like mole people.

Within an hour there were police moving through the tunnels. They were coming from different directions, through different tunnels, towards the center, towards us, like the trackers you see in those old movies, beating the ground, moving the tiger towards each other.

There was nothing we could do but keep moving. Maybe they weren't really in all the tunnels. If they were, which ones? It was impossible to know for sure.

At a certain point we heard voices ahead of us and we stopped and hid. We saw the same two detectives with two other policemen. They were talking with some of the mole people. The big bald detective was barking at one of them, a young man we had seen one of the first days we entered the tunnels.

The young girl I knew was with the women a little way off. They all kept their heads down in front of the police. The young man squatted and held his head down, shielding himself with his arm. Soon we saw the reason why. The big detective struck the young man, pushed him around. Maybe because the young man had dared to look at the fat prick. The other detective, the dark-haired partner, said something, but the big one ignored him. He took the young man by the arm and threw him down an empty elevator shaft. All in one motion. The young man was gone. Just like that.

We couldn't believe it. Jimmy held me tight because I don't know what I would have done – screamed or taken my gun and tried to kill the bastard. If he had moved towards the girl and the other women we would have tried to stop him for sure. We waited. We were always waiting now.

The other detective turned and walked away, and the other police didn't know what to do. The remaining mole people were either crying or silent, terrified. The girl and the other women kept their heads down, not daring to look up. They were crying too.

The big detective turned away from the shaft and said something to the mole people again, only he didn't bark this time. He spoke quietly, like he was sorry, like that was all he needed to do to make things better. The other detective pulled his partner away and they all left. The big detective didn't resist.

We heard a little of what he said at the end when he was talking to the mole people. We knew it was about some reward. And we knew it was about us.

I wanted to live. I had been thinking of surrendering, all of us going in. Not now. If there was ever a chance of that, I knew it was gone. I was sure now that the bald detective would kill us right there if he got the chance.

We couldn't trust anyone. Not anymore. No one. It was just us. For real this time.

We stayed for two days in our last remaining safe place. Waiting. It drove us crazy. I felt trapped in a maze. It seemed quiet around us, but we couldn't be sure. After two days I couldn't stand it down there. I had to get out and learn what was going on in the city. I had to see some kind of light, daylight, city lights, anything.

Jimmy and Kaz came with me. They had to get out too. Kaz was getting silent, moving more into himself. In another day I think he would have snapped.

We worked our way through the tunnels and went up through the old subway station and came out near Gracie Mansion. The city was all about the bombings. It was like a war. There were police everywhere. It was all over the news.

I wanted to go to my family, to see them a last time. Jimmy and Kaz wouldn't let me. I knew they were right. They would be waiting for us. Our families were in enough trouble as it was. I cried, something I regret them seeing. Jimmy and Kaz were good to me, and Jimmy held me close. They understood. We sensed there was no getting out now. It would end soon, one way or another. We had to be good with each other from now on.

I felt something weird then. I wasn't that afraid anymore. Like there was something telling me that it was alright. Not a voice. Not even a feeling. Something, a comfort. It was the first time since we had started that I really believed that whatever happened was OK. There was something moving us along, for a purpose, this time in a good way. Maybe it had something to do with what Jimmy had said, about not fearing anymore. No,

I wasn't that far yet. I still feared death. I couldn't imagine not fearing it. I guess I just accepted it more now.

It wasn't long before we saw the police cars. We entered the tunnels again. Soon we could hear the police behind us. There were a lot of them. They were everywhere. Some carried automatic weapons. I saw the two detectives. The big one held some cloth up to his face, as though he couldn't stand breathing in the air, like it was toxic.

It wasn't long before they almost caught up to us. They told us to stop. We looked at each other and we knew what was going to happen. We knew they would kill us. We kept going. Didn't get out by much that time. They would soon figure everything out. There would be no more places to hide.

Later we sat in a restaurant. The tunnels were too dangerous now. We were so depressed, so alone. It was awhile before we could say anything. I wanted to try and leave the city right away, but Jimmy told me to chill. We would figure it out. He was always angry when he couldn't figure things out, but this time he was really stumped. We were out of ideas. That was weird, to see Jimmy blocked like that.

This was no coincidence, the building, their finding us. Someone knew about us, someone knew. We felt trapped, like we couldn't move. Our world had suddenly collapsed to only a few inches around us.

There were sirens everywhere now. They worked on our nerves. After a while we went back into the tunnels again. Jimmy and Kaz wanted to look, to try and see what had happened. It was weird but we felt safer now down there than in the city. At least there were no sirens.

As we walked through the tunnels we were like sleepwalkers, numb, confused. I know we were all thinking the same thing. We could still somehow get out of this, we could still surface and try and exit. Escape. Maybe there was still a little time. Even Jimmy was thinking it. I could see it in his eyes. We could still run. We could somehow make it.

Then the moment was gone. Men were in the tunnels again. We sat and waited. The voices were still distant but they soon became louder. Jimmy reached behind and took out three pistols from a hidden bag and handed them out. We sat there in the dark and listened. The men were coming along the maintenance tunnel, the same way we had reached the room where we were hiding.

I wanted to whisper something to Jimmy but I couldn't think of anything. None of us wanted to break that silence and the waiting. It was almost like we wanted it to happen, to be over with. Jimmy could sense what I was thinking. He found my hand and held it. It was the first time I had ever felt his hand was cold.

We were in it now.

The men were almost at the room. Jimmy moved his hand away and braced the door with a piece of pipe. We could hear them clearly now. They were loud, too loud for police. No, they were workers, subway maintenance, heading towards the blast. It was almost a disappointment. I believe we were ready to die at that moment. All of us. Ready to just get it over with. I wasn't sure that moment would ever come back.

There was a pause and the door handle turned but the door remained closed. We waited, looking at that handle. One of the men outside said something and moved further along.

Jimmy and Kaz put their hands over the inside part of the handle and held on tight. The door remained closed and the man on the other side stopped trying to open it. Then we heard him move on with the others.

We remained there, waiting. The maintenance room with all the communications connections was at least a hundred yards down the tunnel. They might be back soon. Everything had changed. There would be more police in the tunnel soon with these maintenance men, looking at old maps of the subway and tunnels, maps from the archives. They would soon figure out the best places for us to hide.

After a time we left the room and walked back along the maintenance corridor then into the subway tunnel. The tunnel was clear, some of the trains had stopped working, had shut down. We took the nearest exit to the surface, through another office building and out into the street. We took a cab to Queens and got out several blocks away from the apartment and walked, stopping regularly to look around. We waited a long time near the apartment building. There were no police around. Maybe we had been wrong all along. Jimmy went in and signaled us that it was clear.

We still had our pistols in our coat pockets. The point of my pistol barrel had burrowed through the fabric at the bottom of my pocket. Part of the barrel was sticking out, in plain view. Amateurs. I threw the pistol on the sofa in disgust and threw my coat on the floor. No one said a thing. No one knew what to say.

"We're good and fucked now," I finally said. Someone had to say it. Kaz started laughing. I wanted to hit him again.

I told him to stop laughing. But he kept laughing. I walked over to him to hit him again, but I couldn't. He looked so strange now. So distant. It wasn't Kaz anymore. I thought we were all going mad.

"That's the whole point, isn't it?" Kaz said. "We were fucked when we started."

"Are you sorry about the little boy and the mother?" I asked him. I didn't care if we didn't have anything to do with it. To me, we were just as bad as the ones who had caused the blast.

"No," he said with tears in his eyes. I saw that he meant it. He was trying to piss me off. I raised my arm and he made no attempt to stop me. Jimmy was the one who did.

"You can go now," Jimmy told me. "You can still get away. Leave now, Ann. That's what you want, isn't it?"

So much melodrama. I picked up my coat and made for the door. I hated both of them. They could have each other. I wanted to live, to try and get away from everything we had done, from Jimmy and Kaz, my co-conspirators, my comrades. Yeah, right. How I hated them now.

I called out Jimmy's name. He had turned his back to me and didn't say anything, like I wasn't there. I waited a little but he was still quiet. He was so angry at me, like I had betrayed them. Testing my fucking love and loyalty again, the bastard. So that was it.

I left the apartment building and walked along the street. Away from everything, towards nothing. I was just walking. Somewhere.

It was the last time that Jimmy would test my loyalty, my commitment, my love for him. It was all the same for Jimmy. He could never separate them like I could. Well, fuck him. No more.

When I saw the first police car I hesitated. It could have been about something else, something unrelated. But then a second police car pulled up near the apartment building. Four police officers left the cars. Two entered the building, the other two stayed near the entrance. I recognized the two officers entering the building. The huge bald man and his partner.

I stood there, helpless. I couldn't phone Jimmy and tell them to get out.

I waited. Such a long time. It felt like the whole world was watching and waiting. The two police officers came back out. They had somebody with them, a young man who also lived in the building. A drug dealer. They took the young man away and it was quiet again.

Jesus Christ. Could it have been that easy? I was more scared than ever, but relieved that it had been the drug dealer and not us.

Then I saw Jimmy and Kaz walking towards me. They were smiling. Relieved. I walked up to them and embraced them. All three of us embraced. We didn't say a word. We didn't need to. We were back in the shit again. At least we were in it together.

I knew then that we would die together. Maybe for each other. This was what we had to do. It was clear again. We would take down as much of the fucking system as we could, starting with the nexus. Maybe it wouldn't be much, but it would be something. I was scared, we were all scared, but so what? At least there was some real meaning to our lives. How many fucking people can say that?

There was still nothing about us in the media, nothing more about the bombing in the city. There was no mention of the man in the suit, or the two detectives. Nothing. But there was good news. The little boy was recovering in the hospital with his mother. It was now being said that a gas explosion and an electric fire had caused the destruction. Don't panic, right?

I don't know, it was like we came back from the dead, like we had been given another chance. A clean slate. I even got bold enough to go to the hospital and hand flowers to the nursing staff for the little boy and his mother, like all the other well-wishers in the city. If I got on camera somehow, I really didn't care.

You'd think that something like what we had just experienced would have made us more cautious, would have made us think about what we were doing, but that's not the case. Strange. Like I said, if anything, it had cleared the slate, had made us believe even more in what we were doing, had made us bolder, more determined to learn from our lessons. It was like we had been given some crazy second chance to get it right. I can't tell you why we felt that way. Maybe we're all gamblers deep down. You'd think that this would have been the time to run, to try and start our lives again, you'd think that we'd had enough by then. Go figure.

5
SHOWDOWN

We no longer visited the apartment or the house in Brooklyn. That was done. Way too risky. We got rid of anything that could be traced back to us. It wasn't much to begin with, but we made sure we got rid of it.

We sat at a restaurant in the city, talking about it. It was five days after the explosion at the other building. Two days after we had our big change of heart.

It didn't last long. We knew now we weren't cut out for this. The only thing we were sure of now was that we wanted to live. That was our real ideology now, our true belief. We wanted to go home, but we knew that was impossible now. Now we just wanted to get out of the city. After that, who knows? The revolution was over. Shut tight.

Just one more thing. Jimmy and Kaz first wanted to remove the explosives from the room under the bank. They might be traced to us, they might still self-explode and kill. We had enough of bombs and ideology. They would take them and put them down one of the old elevator shafts. After that, we could leave. It would be over. I told them to please hurry. I would stay there in the restaurant and wait for them. I had no stomach left for the tunnels. We had to get out now. This was it. I tried to convince myself that by doing this one good thing we might be given a chance, that it really wasn't too late.

I prayed. It was all I could do. I prayed we be given a chance. It was the most irrational thing I could think of. Freewheeling again. Maybe this time it would work.

When they left I sat there, watching my hands shake. I was angry at my hands' disobedience. I tried to force them to stop shaking but I couldn't. There was nothing to do but wait again.

A few minutes later two police cars showed up outside. Then an unmarked car showed up. Two guys got out of the unmarked car, checked out the payphone and the people walking by. Then one of them looked across the street towards the coffee shop where I was sitting. It was the big bald guy. I didn't see Jimmy and Kaz anywhere. I wanted to warn them. I wanted them here with me. I was scared shitless.

The men talked to the two policemen, who then drove off in their car. The two cops stayed for a while, looking up and down the street. They talked for a few minutes then they started walking across the street towards the restaurant.

I wanted to cry, I was so scared. And I was angry. They looked so fucking sure of themselves. Why not? They had the whole system behind them. System drones. They knew about us now. No question about it. It was time.

I moved to one of the tables at the back of the coffee shop and waited. The bald guy reached the sidewalk, looked up and down the street and then squinted and looked into the coffee shop. The back door was locked, there was someone in the woman's restroom. There was no way out for me.

I didn't know what to do. I just wished that Jimmy had been with me. The guy moved to the front door, opened it and came in, taking his sunglasses off. I expected him to have yellow eyes. He glanced around the coffee shop. I looked right at him. I knew he was going to come over. I knew it. I had a gun in my pocket. *I have to use it. I have to,* I thought.

The bald man walked right over and sat down across from me. He sat down but didn't say a word. He just looked at me. And I knew that he knew. It's like the whole room sank under my feet.

A woman came over to take his order, and she saw that something wasn't right. She asked me if I'm OK. I didn't say or do anything, I was so afraid. Frozen. So much for any new courage showing up. The man showed her his badge and all the time he was just looking at me. She still wanted to know if everything was OK, and he told her to get him a coffee and to fuck off. She left to get the coffee.

The bald man's partner, the one with the sympathetic eyes, came into the coffee shop. He just stared at me for a second, didn't say a word. Then he went out on the street again.

Then the bald guy leaned closer to me across the table.

"I don't care what you're doing," he said. "I really don't. Neither does my partner out there. I hate this whole fucking city and everyone in it. So does my partner. That's just the way it is. I think we can work together on this."

I told him I didn't know what he meant. My voice was shaking, I barely recognized it as mine. It was the truth. I had no fucking idea what he was talking about, but I knew that he knew. I was so scared.

"We can take you in right now for bombing the building on 21st and killing and maiming those innocent people."

I couldn't breathe. The world suddenly crushed the air out of me. The world knew everything about us. It was magic, sorcery. I didn't say a thing.

I looked out the window of the coffee shop but I didn't see Jimmy or Kaz. I was beyond hope now.

"We don't know if they're gonna come back," the bald guy said. "We have a bet. My partner is the cynical one. He doesn't think they're gonna come back for you. I'm the romantic. I said they will. I think Jimmy will come back for you. The other one, what's his name, Kaz? What kind of name is that? Him I'm not so sure of.

"Look, we can talk about what you and your friends are planning, and maybe we can help each other."

My hand automatically moves to my pocket and the gun, and he notices it without moving his eyes.

"No, I don't think so," he said. "You're not thinking, Ann. You're scared and I can see that. You'd be some idiot not to be scared, in your position. Try and relax and listen. Just relax and listen. OK?"

I nod. I don't trust my own voice. I don't trust my hand even reaching and holding the gun.

"We could just as easily be talking to one of your two friends. You just happened to be here. Or maybe you seem like the most reasonable of the three, I don't know. Ann, are you listening?"

The sound of my name made me stone. I couldn't move. It was like he knew everything about me, my whole life, what I was thinking and feeling, where I would be tomorrow, in an hour, for the rest of my life. Why didn't he just tell me?

At that point he looked out to where his partner was standing on the street. He caught his eye and the partner entered the coffee shop. He ordered a coffee and waited until it was ready then brought it over himself and sat down beside us. He smiled at me. I immediately liked him. Despite where we were and what we were talking about, I liked him. There was something in his look, like he somehow wanted to protect me. It was crazy but that's how I felt at that moment. He made me feel that I wasn't all alone. I would have believed anything at that moment.

"Why don't we just wait a few minutes until the others arrive?"

"They won't come," I said. I didn't want them to. I was all ready to play the martyr.

"Look," the big one said, "you can call them if you want and keep them away, but I think they'll want to hear what we say. We won't stop you, if that's what you want. We could have picked you and your friends up anytime. It's the truth. Like the other night outside the apartment in Queens. I can't tell you how many times before that. You want to call them?"

"I don't have a cellphone," I said. He was reaching for his own cellphone to lend to me.

"What's the number, Ann."

"They don't use cellphones," I said.

The bald guy laughed, shook his head and looked at his partner, who was still staring at me. He put his cellphone back in his pocket.

"Jesus," the bald one said, "unbelievable."

Then the other detective looked away, towards the entrance. I wasn't sure what he was really thinking. The sympathetic eyes didn't look as friendly anymore.

We saw now what he was looking at. In a few seconds Jimmy and Kaz came in and looked around the coffee shop. I didn't know what to do. I was happy to see Jimmy, but I was scared of what these two policemen were planning. The bald police officer turned and waved to them, like they were old friends. Jimmy and Kaz stopped, wondering what to do, weighing the situation. They both looked surprised and concerned although they were trying not to show it. They had walked right back into it.

"C'mon over," the big detective said. "No problem, we're just having a little chat, boys. Just a chat. You're part of this conversation."

The other detective, the one with the nice smile, got up and pulled some chairs over from another table. Jimmy and Kaz went to sit down but he stopped them and patted them down and he said something to Kaz, who said something else that I also couldn't hear. The detective with the nice eyes shrugged then nodded to the other detective and let them sit. He didn't find a gun, or if he did, he didn't let the bald one know.

"I'm detective Mike Copernik," the big one said, "and this is detective John Belden. We don't care what you call us, assholes, pricks, we don't care. We're not gonna see each other for very long anyway. Not gonna be playing canasta with each other, right?

"You've seen us around," he said. "What the fuck do you think we been doing? You couldda been long gone, but here we are." I wanted to tell him that we knew what he was doing, he was in the tunnels killing. We saw him kill that young man.

Jimmy and Kaz didn't say a word. They were just as scared as I was. Jimmy kept looking at me, like his eyes were trying to suck the meaning of all this from me. Good luck.

The bald one smiled, like it was all one good-natured thing. "What the fuck are you kids, Marxists? Anarchists? Goddamn

Shriners? Doesn't matter. I told Ann here that we don't give a shit what you're playing at. All I know is you don't have a fucking chance. Here." He motioned towards the other detective, like he was his lackey. The other detective reached down under the table and pulled out a briefcase. From the briefcase he took out a bunch of papers and put them on the table. It could have been anything, the recipe for chicken kiev for all we knew. None of us reached for the papers. I think we were too afraid, like any movement would shatter any hope we had of getting out of this. I couldn't focus. I was just there, existing for as long as I could. We just knew that they had what they said they had on us, and it was all in that file.

"This is what we have on you already," Copernik said. "It's everything about you and your families. Everything. We have a description of you in the same building after the explosion, we have security tapes of you entering the subway, we have photos of you going into the goddamn communications rooms of buildings. I mean we even have you carrying the explosives in the tunnels. You been very busy.

"It's too easy. Even with a bunch of misguided fucked-up kids like you, who my partner and I really believe are OK at heart. You didn't mean to hurt those people in the building, right? I mean I think you really tried to go out of your way not to hurt anyone. We know that, but you know they're gonna fuck you over in the courts anyway. Because you're terrorists, plain and simple, no matter how you dress it all up. OK, you might really believe in what you're doing. You're not in it for the money, right? And we don't think you're in it for any glory, unless we're missing something here."

"That wasn't us," Kaz said. "That wasn't us who killed that old woman and hurt that boy and his mother at that building three days ago."

Copernik ignored him.

"Funny thing is we probably don't like what's out there any more than you do. Our families have been just as fucked over by this system as you three. Belden here, his father was killed by a hit-and-run driver who didn't go to jail. Got off. His family got dick all for a pension, almost killed them. My mother died of an infection. Health insurance wouldn't cover it. We got nothing but a run around. Told us to go fuck ourselves.

"You think you're the only ones with a grudge against The System? We hate this system. This is what we got from The System." The bald one put the thumb of his right hand between the right middle and forefinger and shook it in front of us.

All this time I could feel Belden's eyes on me again. Was there sympathy for me, for us, there? I couldn't be sure. It had been a long time since he smiled.

"Thing is," Belden finally spoke, "we could work together on this."

"What," Kaz said, "you mean blowing up buildings?"

Copernik laughed.

"Fuck no," Copernik said, motioning towards the old bandage on Kaz's hand. "We don't think you know what the fuck you're doing. We're sure as hell not going to get close to that homemade shit that you're brewing up.

"We know you seen us around. Your friendly neighborhood cops. At the apartment, downtown. Other places. You must've been getting suspicious. You knew it was us. But you didn't run, you just went about your business. I mean we're fucking mystified."

Copernik leaned closer as though he was going to tell us a secret. He seemed disappointed in us.

"We know why you were looking at that building. We're sorry about what happened to your family, Ann. To your father. It's all sad. But you three just killed a grandmother and injured a little boy, his mother and a lot of other people. Who knew that bomb would be that big, right? That's because you're a bunch of amateurs and didn't know what the fuck you were doing. And that's true, ain't it?"

"You exploded that bomb," Kaz said. "It was you. The police."

Copernik lit a cigarette and took his time blowing the smoke up to the ceiling, like one of those old campy movie stars. He was so damn calm, none of us could move. We could just wait. It was his world now, we were just visiting.

"Just curious," he said, ignoring Kaz's words. "What were you trying to do, anyway? I mean we could see revenge on those pricks who made life hard for your families. That we understand. We get the insurance building. But what's with these other places? The other buildings? Yeah, we know about those. What was that gonna do?"

We were silent. It all seemed ridiculous now. It had always been ridiculous. Copernik just shrugged.

"Look, we don't care about the other buildings. We want you to keep doing what you're doing. We want you to be terrorists, or whatever it is you think you're doing. We want you doing just what you're doing. And then we're going to kill you."

I saw Jimmy move a little, as though going for his gun. Belden was also reaching for his gun. Copernik put his hand up and smiled.

"Wait, nobody's gonna get killed. Easy. Here's how it is. This is about to get kicked up to the FBI. Any time now federal agents are gonna come swarming into this city looking for you. It's gonna happen. They'll take everything out of our hands, I mean the New York police force, which we are loyal employees of. Do you see how it works? Once the feds come in they'll have you in no time. They don't have to go far. They're right here in Federal Plaza, they have a counterterrorism division, right here in the city, right in your little play area. Did you know about that?"

We kept silent.

"Here's how it is. My partner and me been the only ones investigating this so far. Nobody in the police department likes the feds. Nobody. We been holding onto this information, everything we have on you, keeping it away from the feds. For now, but not for much longer. It's finding its way to Federal Plaza and somebody soon's gonna say 'terrorist' and they're all gonna jump up and they're gonna yell holy shit and the city and tunnels are gonna be swarming with them. You understand? And those counterterrorist shits are no picnic. I mean they'll fuck both you and your families. They're heartless pricks and they don't give a shit."

"What the fuck are you getting at?" Jimmy said.

Copernik looked at him.

"Don't be a disrespectful little shit," Copernik said, pointing his finger at him. "We're trying to help you here. We got three police cars ready, right around the corner. We let you keep your weapons, including Ann's here. Our bet is you don't really know how to use them, not in something like this. We'd probably kill you before you even reached them."

I realized then that Copernik and Belden were probably looking for tape recorders, not guns, when they patted Jimmy and Kaz down. Maybe they were worried the feds had already gotten to us.

"Even if you're faster than we think you'd be dead in no time. There are three cop cars out there right now. Already mentioned that. Also two snipers. You can't see them. Now they suspect that we're looking at a few drug peddlers here, that's all. You don't show a little more respect, we can have them here in a few seconds. We'll play this the way you don't want us to. So just shut the fuck up."

"It's OK, we're listening," I said. These were not my words. It was like someone else was speaking them. I still wanted to believe there was some way out of this. Any way.

"Alright, let's get to the meat. We're giving you a chance here to forget about all this, what's already happened, a chance to walk away from all this. Like it never happened. Some kids who got in over their heads, who should be given another chance."

Jimmy asked how that was possible.

"Tell us what you have planned next," Copernik said.

None of us said anything.

Copernik removed his gun from its holster and pointed it at me. Belden moved closer to Jimmy and Kaz. Copernik's gun was out before I could see it. I was so stunned I was actually calm. I remember thinking that it was weird, that I knew I should be shitting my pants, but there was something so unreal about it.

"I know it's a little early still for trust," Copernik said. "but we have to start sometime. Weird, huh, having a gun out in the middle of this coffee shop and no one else notices or gives a shit. You'd be surprised how many times that happens in public. The coffee shop girl doesn't know we're cops, she's afraid. But when she gets an opportunity she'll phone the police and they'll be here in a really short time and we'll have to play this straight."

I looked back and saw that the two employees behind the counter were trying not to look at us, but they knew what was happening. Copernik was right. The girl was already slipping to the back with her cellphone out.

"Just tell us what you want," I said.

"In a few seconds she'll be calling," Copernik said.

She was already in the back of the restaurant, out of sight.

"A building on Lexington," Kaz said.

Copernik motioned to Belden, who got up quickly and moved behind the counter to the back. He reappeared a few seconds later, talking into his own cellphone. When he was finished he glanced up and nodded to Copernik.

"OK," Copernik said. "A building on Lexington, what's so special about it?"

"No," Jimmy said. "Tell us why you're doing this."

Copernik smiled patiently, like he was talking to a pain-in-the-ass student. I wasn't sure what he would do next. He was so damn calm. Those people always made me nervous.

"OK, you are a stubborn little prick. How thick are you? We want to be the ones who bag some terrorists. Simple as that. We want our names and faces in the papers, on TV, we want to be the ones who are the heroes."

"Bullshit," Kaz said. "There's more to it than that. Why don't you just turn us in now?"

"Because what have you done? Some shitty buildings, one lousy death, some old lady, some dumb kids from the suburbs who jack off reading commie manifestos. It'd be more embarrassing than it's worth...hell, we might as well give you to the feds right now. Unh-unh, you have to do more and we're not gonna cramp your style. You have to be real fucking terrorists. That insurance building was a good start. So were the others. Jesus, we're trying to help you here achieve your aspirations. Cut us some slack. So again, why this building on Lexington?"

"We believe the building is the central terminus, the hub, of a secret communications company that is working for the government and some big corporations," Kaz said. "They use the building to gather information about everybody, from all the social networking websites. You know, to control us."

It seemed as ludicrous as it sounded.

I saw Copernik and Belden exchange glances, unsure. Then Copernik smiled.

"You're not fucking with us, are you?" Copernik said.

Kaz said we weren't fucking with them.

"We know that building. It's a bank. That's all."

"No," Kaz said, "It's more than that."

"Jesus Christ, you three really are something. What the fuck did your parents do to you?

"Let me tell you something. OK, if you're right, there's no bank there, it's a – what did you call it?"

"A building for gathering information about people, about you and me, Detective," Kaz said, "about all of us."

"And what would that bad company do with all this information about us?"

"Control us."

"You mean like mind control?"

Jimmy told him to fuck off. Copernik reached across, grabbed Jimmy's right arm and pulled it across the table. He brought his gun down on the back of Jimmy's hand. It was a sudden movement. It was surprising how quickly someone that big could move.

Jimmy never made a sound. He cradled his hand and the blood drained from his face. I was sure his hand was broken. I couldn't move. Belden showed his badge to the employees and said it was alright, that we were suspects in an important case. I felt sorry for them. They really wanted to help, but we were in the grasp of The System now. We were lost. Kaz and I sat there, helpless. It was everything I could do not to cry.

"Now that I have your attention, forget that building," Copernik said. "Let me tell you something. That building is a trap. It's meant to attract terrorist wannabes like you, to catch them. Everybody who works there is city police or a fed."

"That's bullshit," Kaz said.

"Yeah? Did you get through the wall and up into the ceiling and the room? Yeah you did, didn't you? It was easy to get in. What did you see in that room?"

Kaz didn't answer him. Copernik turned to Belden and asked him what those things in the room were called. Belden said they were supercomputers.

"Right, supercomputers. And if you had one of those little cameras you saw what? Everything was kinda misty and dark, right, so you couldn't get a good look. Those are dummy computers, everything in there is fake, all the equipment, the whole thing is a honey pot to catch you types. You're the first idiots to bite."

It was like the world had changed completely. We were in a strange land where nothing made sense any more.

"You set the explosives yet on the building?" Copernik asked Kaz.

"It doesn't matter anyway," Copernik said. "Change of plans. We have something else in mind. Something that will make a statement for you, revolution and all that shit, and get us what we want. Everybody wins. You walk away. We want you to come into the tunnels with us. We'll show you. Just one building. We choose it. OK? No bullshit."

Kaz asked what building it was. Copernik only smiled again. I knew then he had it in for Kaz. He had already decided.

"You'll let us go free," I said. I knew there was no way, but I had to say it, as though saying it would make it come true. I had to believe we could get out, somehow. I would have believed a snake oil salesman at that point.

"Yeah, that's right. Do whatever the hell you want. Go start a revolution somewhere else. Nobody will be the wiser. Just this one building."

"You said before that we would be killed," Kaz said.

Copernik laughed. His whole body shook. It shook the table. "Yeah, you will be. Only it won't be you. Don't worry about that now. That's our problem. You have one minute to decide. So decide."

I was hoping that one of us would have the courage to try for our guns and kill the both of them, or be killed, right there. But we didn't. We might as well have been statues. We were trying to buy some time, to think of something to get us off this hook. That was the trouble, we were always thinking, buying more time. Look where it got us.

I saw Copernik and Belden exchange glances again.

Copernik nodded at him then got up from the table and walked over to one side of the restaurant, where he made a call on his cellphone.

We could have made a run for it right there. It was probably lies, about cop cars waiting out there with snipers. We couldn't see any cars from where we were sitting. Where would the snipers even be? In what buildings? Hiding behind some dumpsters? What fools we were. Children.

Belden stared at his fingernails and occasionally looked at Copernik, at the restaurant, at the employees. He kept looking back at the door as though expecting someone, but no one came in. A strange thought crossed my mind. I wondered how this place stayed in business without customers. Maybe it was all a front for the cops. You never know. Anything had become possible in that restaurant.

I looked at Jimmy, but I couldn't tell what he was thinking. I was angry at him, at us. It was like we had never communicated before, and the one time we really needed it, Jimmy just sat there, avoiding my eyes. I hated him. We sat there and waited, scared. We waited for some miracle to save us. It would be a long fucking wait.

Copernik returned. He was all business now, a car salesman ready to take us out to look at the new models.

"It'll only take a few minutes," Copernik said. "Why don't we at least go look at it?"

"You mean now?" Kaz said.

"I mean now."

"What about the feds?" Jimmy asked. "If what you say about the building is true, they'll know about what we're doing."

"That won't be a problem. I don't even think they would know yet. This might work. Let's go. We'll show you this place. Let's get to your place at Lexington first. Let's see how you rigged this stuff. I'm sorry about your hand, kid."

Something had changed between Copernik and Belden, a new plan was forming. Something on the go. They had found some kind of new opportunity. Whatever it was, it still wouldn't be good for the three of us.

They wanted something before the feds got to it. Us. And I didn't think it meant us staying alive.

Copernik and Belden led us into the subway through a door in an underground parking garage on Madison. We made our way through the tunnels beneath Lexington. None of us knew about this entrance at the parking garage. It scared us that these others knew everything about us. There was nothing they didn't know. Nothing was a secret anymore. We were like children.

Copernik suddenly put his gun to Kaz's head.

"This is only going to work if we have trust, right?"

I saw Belden move towards Copernik. It was only a second, but it gave me hope that maybe he had some doubts about all this. I caught Belden's eye for a moment, until he turned away. He was not sure. Something had changed and he didn't like it. I wasn't sure if Copernik saw it too.

"In the maintenance room there's an old vent that leads into the building," Jimmy said. "We saw it on some old schematics."

It was all lies. I couldn't tell what Jimmy was up to. It was some kind of stall.

"It used to be part of an old bank branch, Manhattan Trust, a hundred years ago," Kaz said. "The vent stops about six feet away from the building. Workers walled up that section in the fifties after the bank went bust. There's a hollow section beyond the first cement block wall and the wall of the building. On the other side of that wall is the communications room.

There's a shitload of computers in there. I saw them. They're real. I'm positive."

Kaz had picked up on Jimmy's lies and was running with them.

Copernik and Belden talked.

Then Copernik told us to move on. Maybe he was wondering now if what the feds had said about the nexus building, about the computers, was a lie.

There was no argument about it. He told us to keep going. We didn't argue. We were too tired. It all seemed so inevitable now. We weren't afraid. That was the weird part. We had few emotions left. We were all just thinking about death now. And we all knew from the start that it would lead to this. It was now, and not then, not some other time. That was all.

Copernik didn't believe a word of what we were saying. He pulled me over to him.

"No trust. It's a pity. Remember this, they would never find her down here. C'mon, you know that. Take us to the fucking building and show us."

Kaz said we were there. He pointed to the strange concrete structure.

"This is the bank under Lexington?" Copernik asked and let me go. "Show me."

Kaz took him over to the door and they went inside. They were in there for an eternity but I know it was only a minute. We didn't hear anything. It was all quiet, just some rumbling of a train in the distance. I looked at Belden a few times. He wasn't looking anywhere. What was going on? I looked at Jimmy and he had this set expression and his eyes looked past me, they looked hard at Belden, and I knew then.

Only Copernik came out again.

Jimmy went for his gun but Belden knocked him down. Jimmy didn't move for a few seconds. Belden took Jimmy's gun and gave it to Copernik. They got mine also. Copernik came over and kicked Jimmy hard. I came at Copernik and he knocked me down. He was strong, so strong. It was like hitting a wall.

"I think this will do," Copernik said to Belden. "We have some time before the others get here."

I looked at Belden. I couldn't tell what he was thinking. It was maddening. Jimmy was hurt but I could see that he was breathing.

"Go in to see your friend," Copernik said, motioning towards the metal door. "He doesn't have much time."

I helped Jimmy get up and we went towards the door, but Copernik told Jimmy to stop. Only I was to go in. I don't know why.

Kaz was lying on his side. His head had been cracked open. He looked at me and seemed surprised to see me. He smiled. He knew he was dying and he wanted to make his peace. Like I was some kind of priest. He was anxious to tell me everything. Now, when he was dying, he wanted to open up.

"Vecchio, I told him about the tunnels. Before we went down. He must have known it was us. I think he went to the police for the reward," Kaz told me.

"I know," I lied, "I know. It's OK. It wouldn't have made much difference. Not now." I didn't tell him that it wouldn't have mattered, even if Vecchio hadn't been around. The System had known all about us, for some time. With or without Vecchio.

He seemed pleased with my reaction, like it was some kind of expiation for his sins.

"You always hated me, Ann." His words were matter-of-fact. A scientist to the end.

"That's not true," I told him. Maybe it was.

"No, it's OK. I understand."

He placed his fingers over my hand. His fingers were already like ice. It was all I could do not to pull my hand away.

"Jesus, what a prick I am," he said. "I'm so sorry."

"It's OK."

He looked at me, an agonizing look that said he was sorry and was asking for forgiveness. This was it. I knew he was waiting for it. He wasn't going to get it. Not from me. Not now. Not ever. I wouldn't forgive him.

"What about Jimmy?" he asked. I'm not even sure he knew where he was anymore. I told Kaz that Jimmy would be here in a minute. I lied. I didn't want Jimmy to see him. I didn't want Jimmy to forgive him. I wanted Jimmy to hate him, like me.

It didn't matter anymore. Something was washing over him now, and it was taking everything that was still left of Kaz with it.

Truth is I hated him at that moment, even with him dying I wanted to smash his face in. I wanted to keep him away from Jimmy, once and for all. I'm not ashamed of it. Maybe it would have made a difference, that damn building. Maybe Jimmy and I could have gotten out, lived. Maybe we could have been up in the air again above these tunnels together. We'd never know now. We'd never leave these fucking tunnels.

"I betrayed us," he said slowly, with a final bit of energy, as though I was a child and didn't have the brains to understand. "Don't you get it? I fucking betrayed us."

What did he want from me? Forgiveness? Did he want me to finish him off? Fuck him and fuck Vecchio. That was like Kaz, right to the end. He never thought anybody else could really get it. Not like him. Not like Jimmy. Only they could get it.

He looked past me for a second, at what I'm not sure. Maybe he saw that other thing that was always with us. That thing that hated us. Maybe it had come for him. I even looked around, but I didn't see anything else in that room. It was just us. When I turned back Kaz was still, no longer moving. It took me some time to understand that he was dead. Gone. I looked through Kaz's pockets and around the room. There was nothing like a weapon there. Copernik had taken it. I could only think of survival then. There was nothing else.

Then Jimmy came in. The time dragged on. Jimmy and I held each other. I could feel Jimmy crying inside. Would he cry as much for me? I didn't want him to go for Copernik because of Kaz. I'm ashamed to say I felt like it would be a betrayal on Jimmy's part. I just wanted to hold onto Jimmy as long as I could. He was really hurt and his breathing was bad. I thought that Jimmy's ribs were broken.

I was waiting for the door to be shut and for us to be trapped inside, but after a minute Copernik appeared and told us to come out again. I was hoping that whatever mysterious force moved in those tunnels, those urban legends, sweeping bodies away, would also have taken Copernik. Maybe he was just too big and too fat to be taken. Even by the supernatural.

"Did you make your peace with your friend?" Copernik asked. "I'm not a complete prick. It's just that he didn't commit to trust. He disrespected me. He disrespected me, you understand?

"And it was your friend who fucked you up. You should thank me."

Copernik looked at his watch and walked around the corner of the tunnel and looked and listened. Was he waiting for somebody?

I tried to make conversation with Belden. I felt that he was our only hope. I told him what he already knew, that his partner was going to kill us. But he didn't respond. I was too nervous anyway. He knew what I was doing. Trying to get his trust. It was pathetic. On looking back, I'm not sure some of it didn't work.

Copernik came back and laughed. "I think she likes you, John," he said.

Belden seemed restless and walked off to explore some of the tunnels. Now that I think of it, I believe he went to make up his mind about what he was going to do a short time later. Copernik told him not to go too far, it was easy to get lost. There was sarcasm in his words. Copernik then took my gun and held it in front of me.

"You had your chance back at the restaurant, and you know it, don't you, little girl? And you, Jimmy. You three, how did you expect to get anywhere with this shit when you don't even see an opportunity in front of you?

"I mean this is too easy for us. I almost feel sorry for you. You really are just dumb kids." He smiled.

He told us he used to explore these tunnels when he was a kid. He knew them a lot better than we did. He said he knew more hiding places than we could imagine.

That made my heart sink even more.

What were they waiting for? Why were they waiting to kill us?

"Lots of people disappear down here, another one or two are not gonna make any difference. There's nothing here," he said, pointing into the dark. "Tunnel doesn't lead anywhere. This is the old Manhattan Trust building. There's nothing weird about it. Your friend Kaz was a fucking moron. Tell me, do you really love each other, you and Jimmy?"

"There was never any other building," I said. "You were never going to let us go. You're going to kill us here and that'll be it."

"You're smarter than your two friends, Ann. And don't think Belden will help you. Sorry. We're old buddies, since we were kids. He knows these tunnels better than me."

"You'll kill us here, won't you?" I said. Enough bullshit. I just wanted him to finally admit it.

"Just as you were about to blow this old building. We've already scoped it. It's perfect, just waiting. Too bad. Together we couldda have done some real damage to this town."

We sat there in silence for some time. He kept looking into the tunnel behind me, waiting for Belden to return. I could sense that he wasn't as sure as he sounded.

"Tell me why you were doing this, Ann. It must look pretty stupid right about now. I don't think you were as dedicated to whatever you were doing as your friends. Am I right? Nice kid, just a bit fucking naïve. Isn't that right, Ann? You getting mixed up with these two fucking idiots."

"Leave her alone, Mike," Belden said. He had appeared from one of the other tunnels. Copernik didn't answer him. He raised his eyes and gave his partner a sharp look then ignored him.

"Alright Ann, I think you know what's gonna happen here. You saw us that time, at the old elevator shaft. This is nothing for us. All you have to do is tell us where the money is. That's all. Just tell us and we're done here."

"There's no money," Jimmy said. "You know that."

Copernik knew that. It was never about the money.

"Jesus, Mike," Belden said. Copernik told him to keep watching the tunnel. "Fucking dumb spic," Copernik muttered under his breath. There was now some venom in his voice.

"You knew about this place," I said. "You knew what we were doing here. You were watching."

I had already resigned myself to death. His threats suddenly meant nothing. I couldn't think, I couldn't see any way out now. Death was death, right? Whether for a noble cause or just seeing it out, being done with it. It didn't matter anymore. That was the end, nothing more, a dark well. Nothing more. I was ready. At least I wouldn't have to listen to this windbag anymore. The dark and quiet would be a relief.

He asked me again, about why we did what we did. I still didn't answer. I couldn't anyway. It seemed so strange to me now. Why did he want to know so much? What were we doing this for? I couldn't tell you then. I'm not sure I can tell you now. It was a silly game. Just surviving seemed like the most important, noble thing we could do. Even that seemed empty. It was hopeless. I didn't try to reply. He never expected a reply anyway. What was he waiting for?

"Here, I want to show you something."

He dragged me towards some subway maintenance equipment piled nearby. On the other side there were two long green things that looked like cocoons. Copernik opened one of them. It was the body of a young man. He looked like he was Middle Eastern. In the other bag was a young woman. She also had dark skin. I wasn't sure what to think. I couldn't think. These could have been strange tunnel creatures they had bagged.

"These are what they want," Copernik said, "not you or Jimmy. You two don't exist anymore."

Then he asked me again. He didn't care about my answer. Or maybe there was something inside him that really wanted to know. I think he just needed to be obeyed. When I didn't answer he took my arm and twisted it. He wanted me to tell him that we did it for the most noble of reasons; it would make it more important when they killed us. It would make it more noble for him. Or maybe he wanted me to tell him that we had been fools, then it would make it more right for them to kill us. Either way it didn't matter anymore. I was still silent. I wasn't going to give Copernik what he wanted. He could kill me first.

This time he brought his gun down on my arm. I cried out. It felt like the arm from the elbow up would shatter. I sank to my knees but he still held my arm. He wanted to see me cry, like that was proof of what I deserved. Like that was some kind of justice.

Jimmy reached for Copernik, who knocked him down again. I hoped he would stay there.

Copernik pulled me up by the arm. "C'mon, I'll show you something else."

He dragged me towards the abandoned elevator shaft and held me over it, bending my head forward like he wanted me to look. I closed my eyes and waited. Somehow it was better with the eyes closed. A short sensation of flight for a few moments and then nothing. It would be over quickly.

I didn't hear anyone else at first. I only heard Copernik, angry, and I thought he was angry and shouting at me. Copernik let my arm go and when I looked up someone was on the other side of the elevator shaft with his gun pointed at Copernik. It was Belden. I didn't move.

Belden didn't say a word.

"Fuck, doesn't anybody say anything anymore?" Copernik screamed.

If Belden had said something, it would have been different. But he didn't. Maybe he knew that even a few words would be disastrous, I don't know. He just stood there staring at Copernik, his eyes steady on him as if it was all inevitable. It infuriated the big detective. Then he tried to talk through it.

"John, what's this about?" He sounded a lot friendlier, but there was menace in his voice.

Copernik told me not to move.

Shoot him, I thought. The more he talks the more dangerous he is. Shoot him. Just fucking kill him. I wanted to live. I wanted Jimmy and me to live.

"You think I'm gonna kill her? You're not falling in love with her, are you, you big romantic spic? Why would I kill her? I'm trying to scare her. That's all. Just a little. Look, she's all ready to die, she's mumbling, her lips are moving, she's praying. Hey little girl, do you pray? Little revolutionary girl?"

He pushed my head down until it felt like the neck would snap. I didn't want to open my eyes, though I could sense the open space below me. I wanted to look.

I could hear him take his gun from his pocket behind me. I wanted to warn Belden but I couldn't say anything, I knew that he would drop me, I was suddenly terrified of that space below. Did Belden see what was going on? It was a play being acted out behind the curtain, I could only see shadows moving.

I didn't see what happened. I only heard two shots. Then another. Please, I thought. Please. When I looked up again Belden was almost dead, lying on his side. Copernik walked over to his partner and knelt beside him and took his gun. I saw my gun in Copernik's other hand.

"Jesus, John," Copernik said softly, shaking his head. "I wasn't gonna kill her. Honest. You fucking idiot. Look what you done." Belden was no longer moving. His eyes got that fixed look, like they were set and never going to move again. Just like Kaz's eyes.

Copernik looked back at me. His eyes were cold with hate. He looked at his watch then turned my gun on himself and shot himself through the left arm. He wiped the gun clean on his shirt then came back to me and twisted my arm again forcing my hand open. He put the gun in my hand and squeezed my fingers around it then backed away and dropped the gun near the elevator shaft.

He kicked Jimmy, who woke up and immediately looked for his gun. He told Jimmy to get up. I helped Jimmy get to his feet. He was all wobbly. I'm not even sure he knew where he was.

"Now run," Copernik said.

At first I thought he would shoot us right there.

"Fucking run! I'm giving you a chance. Don't ever tell me I'm not a romantic. Run!"

We started to walk slowly down the tunnel. I expected bullets to hit us any second. I closed my eyes and waited, just like at the elevator shaft. The pain then sleep. It wasn't so bad.

We tried to run but Jimmy could barely walk. He put his head on my shoulder, rested some of his weight against me. At a certain point I looked back. Copernik was standing over Belden's body. He was waiting. I knew he was waiting for the police. I remembered that call he made on his cellphone before we left the restaurant. He had told them to wait until now, before they entered the tunnels towards us.

We moved blindly. I didn't know where I was going, I just followed the tunnel. I wanted to live. I wanted us to live. Maybe there was a chance as long as we kept moving. In a short time we saw two people ahead. The police. We squeezed our bodies into a small recess against the wall and waited. There was no escape. They would find us in a few seconds.

We could hear them coming. Copernik's voice. He would be telling them how dangerous we are, how Belden never had a chance. How they found us on a hunch. It was good police work. He would tell them what we were planning. It would be useless trying to take us alive. Maybe he didn't have to tell them, maybe they were all involved. There wouldn't be any chance of getting out alive. It was never an option.

The police passed us. Were we dead already, ghosts? They weren't looking for us, not yet. They just stared ahead, into the tunnel. It was an alien environment for them. Another planet. The air and the sounds were different, confusing to their senses. That was good. We kept moving. We didn't know where, just away from them and not towards any others.

We saw some of the mole people on the way. We asked for help but they turned away from us. They were afraid of the police. They told us to move on. They just disappeared. They wouldn't even give us some of their medical supplies. They were terrified of Copernik and the others. They wanted us gone forever. They wanted us all gone. I didn't see the little girl with them. Was she alright? They wouldn't tell me. They didn't want to give us any information. To them, we were just as bad as Copernik. I hoped they wouldn't help the police, for the reward. A few of them gave us some food, others looked at us with sympathy and wished us luck, but they wanted us to keep moving.

We reached one of our storage spaces, the old locker near the abandoned station. Sounds echoed everywhere in the tunnels. It was so hard to pinpoint directions. We could hear them coming though, from both sides. It was useless.

We tried one more time to make it up to the city. We crouched and moved through some of the conduit cable tunnels and we could see a little daylight when we reached the end. We could see a window, some people moving around. It was starting to get dark. I recognized it. It was just outside Rockefeller Plaza. We had been there before, when we were exploring under the city. I remembered a small door. If we could just get on the other side of it. It was locked. We tried everything to open it, but it was hopeless. Jimmy was getting tired and because of the injury to his ribs he had trouble getting any kind of pressure against it. I was not strong enough.

It was weird, we could see people moving around out there on the street, walking, hurrying home from work, we could see their faces. One of them even dropped something and looked right at us when she picked it up, but I don't think she saw us. We could have been a million miles away.

I went back along the conduit tunnels, making sure we didn't miss anything, any exit doors, but it was like everything had changed in the last few months. I came across some workers and turned back to get Jimmy. There was nothing more to do but go back into the tunnels.

We never made it to the next exit. There were police coming from all sides. I could sense it. They had no intention of taking us alive.

When we reached the room in the heating vents, we stopped. I tried to help Jimmy climb up to the mattresses in the pipes, but he kept slipping. He didn't have the strength to make it. We tried again and he finally was able to boost himself to the lower mattress.

We lay there, as quiet as possible, just the sounds of the hot water moving through the pipes, the sounds getting louder then softer in waves. In a few minutes we could hear the police outside the room. One of them came in and looked around. I looked down at Jimmy through the pipes. He was covered in sweat and was having trouble breathing. It was hot in that room, hotter than I remembered. They must have turned the heat up in the building above us because of the colder weather. Jimmy smiled up at me through the pipes, but I could see he couldn't last long. He lay there clutching his side in pain. How long did it take that damn policeman? There was nothing there. Why was he waiting? And then I saw it, on the floor. A map that Kaz had made of this section of the tunnels. The one Kaz had given to me when we first entered the tunnels. I must have dropped it. The policeman picked it up and studied it. I could see he was trying to put it together. But it could have been from anyone, one of the mole people, maybe one of the maintenance workers.

The policeman looked up into the pipes. I moved back and was still. I snaked my hand down past a pipe towards Jimmy and he reached up and took my hand. His hand was so cold and wet, it was a shock. He had always been so warm. It was so ominous how cold his hand felt. We waited. When I couldn't stand it anymore I moved to my side and peeked down through the pipes. Jimmy put his finger to his lips. Beyond him I could see part of the man below. It was the same man in the suit whom we had seen before. He was staring up into the pipes, trying to make sense of something that was bothering him. Something was up there that didn't make sense. He must have seen part of the mattress where Jimmy was lying. I scrunched around a little on my side and lifted the gun with my right hand. But I couldn't move my arm around to use the gun. I didn't dare move again. Jimmy smiled at me and shook his head for me to wait. I closed my eyes and waited. I knew he was looking right up at us. It was only a matter of time, a few seconds. Maybe he thought it must be too hot for anyone to be up there. He started to climb up. Then I saw a large drop of condensation form on the pipe near me. It grew bigger and finally dropped. It cleared the pipes and I could hear it hit the man in the suit in the face. He cursed and turned and wiped his face and left to join the others.

We stayed there for several minutes more until we were sure they were gone and then I helped Jimmy climb down. There was some water stored in a container nearby. We drank it all. I saw now that I had burned the skin near my wrist and on my fingers. Jimmy's palms were burned but it wasn't severe. We couldn't stay there. We saw it was clear and moved on.

We hid in the little room that had been shown to me before by the girl in the tunnels. We had stored some of the medical supplies there. We hid there for a long time. I'm not ashamed to say that I was terrified. I put some cream on our burns and tried to wrap bandages around our hands, but it was no good.

We talked for a long time in that little room. Jimmy was already planning our revenge on Vecchio, but these were empty words and we knew it. Jimmy was hurt about what Kaz did with Vecchio. We both were. There was only the two of us now. We could only trust each other. We talked about what we were doing, how it was still important, how we never expected it to end any other way. Empty words again. Now that it was happening, I was numb. It couldn't really be happening, I never thought it would end this way. Not really. Not yet. I couldn't accept it. No more bullshit philosophy. I didn't care about The System. It could go on for a thousand years and spawn other systems, I didn't give a shit. Only survival, that's all that still mattered.

Jimmy's breathing became worse. We couldn't stay in that little room. It felt like a tomb. I needed to breathe, to act. I looked at Kaz's maps again.

One of the maps showed something else, a vent not too far away. If we could get to it, maybe there was a chance. We left the room and walked as fast as we could but it was so dark. We could hear them getting closer and then there were shots and Jimmy just collapsed. He held my arm and then let go and told me to run. I tried to lift him to his feet but he fell back.

Then he got up and we started to walk again. We took a side tunnel and made it to one of the maintenance doors. I knew Jimmy couldn't go on. We went inside and we waited and then we heard them moving away into one of the other tunnels. It was dark inside that room, we couldn't see a thing. I only had some matches. The light only lasted a few seconds. There was blood coming out of Jimmy's left leg. He had also been hit in the back. He was shielding me when he was hit. He fell in that room and stayed down and I couldn't get him up again.

I only had a small piece of cloth. We wrapped that around the leg wound but I couldn't get it tight enough because of my burns.

I didn't know what to do but Jimmy calmed me down and I said that I would go and try and get to the storage space under 48th Street, where we had some more medical supplies. I knew it wouldn't be enough to stop the bleeding.

Jimmy told me to stay. But I was desperate, I said I would go into the city and talk to one of my friends who had once been sympathetic to radical causes and who was now a medical intern at one of the city hospitals and he could come down and get Jimmy patched up and better. I honestly believed it could happen. I had to.

But Jimmy only smiled and caressed my cheek. What I was saying was crazy of course. It was over. He knew it and was waiting for me to catch up to it. Our bodies sagged together into a kind of calm defeat. There was nothing more.

"Don't be upset," he said. "We knew this was going to happen." He wanted me to be brave, to nod and say it was all worth it, he was begging me, but I couldn't do it. His words sounded so empty to me.

My heart was saying that it was all a waste, all madness, that I didn't want any of this to happen, that I cursed whatever brought us together again to do this insane thing. But I stayed silent.

We told each other that we loved one another, that it wouldn't be the last time we would see each other, that we would be together again. We talked all that bullshit bourgeois schmaltz, everything that we laughed at and hated before and it made me even more furious because it seemed to mock us and tell us that everything we believed in was fake, that we were just like everyone else. Worse. We were hypocrites.

It didn't matter. There was no talk about philosophy, The System, only about us now. I was glad. That's all that mattered now. There was nothing more.

The last match light went out and we sat there with our bodies together in the dark. I was crying, I couldn't help it, and he comforted me and told me that it was OK and that he just wanted us to be together in the calm stillness at the end. We didn't say a word after that and after some time I could feel his breathing get weak and his arm relax around me. I don't think he could hear my crying anymore.

I just hoped that I could be as calm as he was at the end.

I stayed with him a long time, there in the dark. He finally fell asleep. Then I went along the tunnels to the medical supply space and brought some back, along with some explosives and an extra gun that Jimmy had hidden there. I was dead, you see, out of my mind, it was the last thing I remembered. But I had to do something. I couldn't stand the waiting. That's the way it always is with me. I had to do something, to keep moving.

I went up to the surface, to the city. I went through the same parking garage, thinking that they wouldn't be looking for me there. I went to an apartment building on 43rd Street and phoned up an old college friend. Her roommate answered and asked me to leave a message. I told her it was urgent. She told me that she was at a restaurant around the corner.

I found her there with her boyfriend, another radical type. I didn't care how I looked, how the others were looking at me. I was desperate. She was shocked to see me. And she wasn't happy, like I was some bill collector who had tracked her down. She led me out to the street. She was really embarrassed. I apologized and told her what had happened. I told her everything. I didn't care anymore. This woman was a radical in college. We had been good friends then. She would understand.

When I was finished she asked me what I expected her to do. I hadn't spoken to her in a long time and I just show up here and what did I expect her to do? I didn't know myself. I had no idea. I was shocked at what she was saying to me. I just stared at her.

What could I expect? We were rogue terrorists, operating outside the usual channels by choice, as arrogant and entitled and self-blessed as any of the other bourgeois pricks in The System. We were dangerous to legitimate groups like the one she belonged to, groups who wanted change too, who worked within The System to get it done. She knew all about us. Was there anybody who didn't, I thought?

She gave me a fucking earful. We deserved what was coming to us. We were like dangerous animals. Uncontrollable. She was glad we were done for. We would be forgotten in a few days. I was lucky. She told me if I went to some of the other groups for help they might even kill me right then and there. They were not a peace movement like her friends. She was being kind, you see.

No, there was nothing to be done. I had made my choice, so had Jimmy. We were outside her system and the kinds of groups she belonged to. It was our choice to be outside it. She wasn't going to put herself and the others she knew in jeopardy. How dare I come to see her for help? What did we expect? We were paying for our selfishness, our not playing the game, ignoring the rules, paying for our isolation. Who did we think we were, trying to leave The System?

I didn't know what to say. I could have told her that she and her friends had become just as bad as what they thought they were fighting, even fucking worse than The System, fucking hypocrites, but I didn't care. It wouldn't have made any difference. They were already sleepwalking and they would be pissed if you tried to wake them up. No, they just wanted to keep walking, keep sleeping. Let them.

I asked her instead to forgive me, told her that I really needed help. My friend was dying. That's all that mattered right now. I knew that there were doctors in her group, members that she could call for help. I was begging for her help.

She really gave it to me then. God, she said. Yeah, now this radical was throwing God at me, like He would be judging me too. Pick a fucking number. God, what did I do, what was I doing to my family, to everyone I knew? As for my friend dying, that was too bad, but hey, two members of their group had been killed in protests in Europe last week. For a just cause, she added, something that was organized, well thought-out, something that had a chance of making a real difference, of succeeding. What we were doing only made it more difficult for them, for all those who belonged to real legitimate causes. It would cause more heat, make it easier for the right-wing extremists to make their case against them. We fucked it up for them. There was nothing they could do for us. We were more dangerous than The System. Any day.

She was getting all worked up. Funny, she was real quiet in college, a real bookworm, couldn't get her to say anything. And now she was giving me a real lecture, couldn't get her to shut the fuck up.

I said again to forget about this other shit. I was pleading with her as a friend. That's all. As a friend. To help.

Then she told me that she hoped I was caught, so I would be off the streets, that my friend would die, and make it easier for all of them, for those radicals who counted. Then she got her cellphone out and started dialing. She was calling the police. She was really calling the fucking authorities. I couldn't believe it. She was no better than Copernik and all the other drones.

Her boyfriend came out just as I hit her across the face. He stopped, wondering what was going on, wondering what to do. That really did it. I was done now. She continued making her call. Making sure I heard everything.

The boyfriend asked us what was wrong. He was trying to make sense of it.

I ran. When I looked back, she was going back into the restaurant with her boyfriend. I don't know if she finished making that call or if it was all a bluff. I didn't wait to find out. I didn't hear any sirens, didn't see any police cars. Maybe she just wanted to scare me. Maybe that would be enough.

The boyfriend turned around and came out from the restaurant again. I could see that he was arguing with my friend. Then he looked along the sidewalk towards me and called out something that I couldn't hear or understand. He called out again and then I started to come back. Maybe there was hope. Then I saw my friend say something to him again and they both went back into the restaurant. I didn't go back. I turned around and left. I was too afraid that it was a trap and that they would turn me in.

I hardly knew where I was walking. Time was everything now. There was so little of it.

I had one more place to try. Another old friend from college. I was terrified now, didn't know what to expect. The past, the present, the future, all of it seemed to be full of hatred, watching me.

When I reached my friend's apartment building, I rang up. A woman's voice asked me who I was. I told her I was a friend. She was suspicious. There was silence and then she broke off. I leaned against the wall by the speaker. I didn't know what else to do. The elevator door opened and a woman walked out towards me. She was in her late twenties, like me, nice hair, nice clothes, not like me. I could see in her eyes that she was afraid. Did she know about me? No, how could she? Then I realized how I must have looked. I took the loose bandage from my hand and stuffed it into my pocket. My clothes were stained with sweat and grime. She hesitated then opened the door and let me into the lobby. We just stared at each other. There was nothing to say. There was no pity in her eyes, now not even fear. Just that distance between us. She could have been looking at me across the Grand Canyon.

"Do you need help?" she asked. There was more sympathy in her voice than I expected.

I said I did. If I said any more I knew I would start crying.

She told me my friend was at Langone Medical Center on First Avenue. I knew where it was. I thanked her and left. I know what I was to her. That's why she came down. She was curious. I was the walking dead and she wanted to see what a dead person looked like. She wanted to see how far her husband had come since his days with me. He had come far. I was that cautionary horror tale of what could have been. She must have had the same feeling that people have after a close encounter with death. That sense of relief.

I found my friend at the hospital, talking to some other interns in the cafeteria. It was the first time I had seen him since college.

She hadn't phoned to warn him. I must have looked that pathetic to her. He was surprised to see me, embarrassed. He had changed, I saw it right away. He was always talking before, in college, how he hated The System, how he wanted to do something about it, become a doctor and fight it, like Che Guevara, like Bethune. He had joined the radicals in college, just like me, the same group that the woman who had lectured me belonged to. He left the group after I did. His eyes had been so kind and understanding then. Now they were cold and angry and distant. He hustled me away from the others, out of sight, into one of the conference rooms. I begged him for help, I told him that a friend was in trouble, in desperate need of medical attention, that he had been shot. And then I saw it was hopeless. I was just going through the motions. I expected so little now.

He told me they had come to see him, to question him about me. He had nothing to tell them. Would he have told them if he did know something? How did they even know about us? It seemed like everybody knew, that the world had now only one purpose, to find us. He looked at me with such hatred. In his world now I was the enemy, a threat. Not them. Me.

I was sad to see he was afraid of me, though he was trying hard not to show it. I was as alien and pathetic to him now as any of the druggies and whack jobs he saw every day at the hospital. I could see him searching me over with his eyes, looking for weapons, maybe for drugs, any other shit that now disgusted him. Things I don't remember disgusting him in college. Well, fuck him and The System.

He told me to wait and left. I was nervous. To the doctors and nurses I must have looked like any other junkie hanging around. I didn't know what my friend would do.

He returned with some bandages and painkillers in a plastic bag.

"Use any kind of clean padding and apply pressure to the wounds, try and elevate him if you can. Is it any kind of chest wound?"

I told him it wasn't. It was my voice, but it was so distant and strange again. He opened the bag and showed me some tampons. I wasn't sure what they were for. I wasn't sure if it was all a joke and I was supposed to laugh. I was helpless.

"These work temporarily, believe me, just put them in the bullet holes as far as they'll go. They'll at least stop the bleeding. Give him these painkillers first. Give him four or five. And get him to a fucking hospital, Ann. Where is he?"

I told him. I didn't think he would call anyone. I didn't think he would trap me. I would have told him anything then. We have to trust at some point, right? Desperation is as right a time as any. This was it. I was all trusting.

His eyes had become softer, more like I remembered. He wrapped the bandage more securely around my hand. I told him how gentle his touch was, that he would make a good doctor. I didn't know what I was saying anymore. Words just came out on their own. I could only listen to them. All bullshit.

"He'll die of infection down there, Ann. There's some iodine in there. It's old school but it works. The nearest hospital from where he is is Metropolitan, OK? You love this guy?"

I told him I loved Jimmy. I would have told him I despised him if it got me more medicine for Jimmy.

"Then get him to Metropolitan, quick."

He asked me what had happened to me. It was all just talk then, he said, it was never really serious, right? Look what it did to my life, he said, and to my family. I was getting another fucking lecture, a quieter one.

I didn't answer. His eyes had gone cold again. I wanted to tell him that it was never just words for me, never just about talk, about getting laid, about growing up, about growing out of it.

What was the point? He had his career, his calling, his car, his path. He was already a dedicated shill for The System. Maybe he always had been. Maybe we all are. What happened to Bethune, to Guevara? I didn't ask him. I didn't care.

I thanked him for the bandages and pills and I left him and the hospital. It worked. He got me angry and focused again. Maybe that's what he wanted. I never looked back. I don't think he did either. I was back in his blind spot. Forever. And he was in mine.

Then I felt a hand on my arm. It was the Doctor.

"Take me to him," he said.

I asked him if he was sure. He said that he was. I told him that I didn't want to get him in trouble. He never answered me. He told me not to worry about it. That's what he used to tell me in college, not to worry about it. There was something reassuring in hearing that again. Maybe there was hope. Something could still be done. Nothing was ever really over.

He asked me if I trusted him. I told him I did. He told me to wait in one of the conference rooms then he came back for me and we left the hospital. We entered the tunnels through the same maintenance room.

I could see he was scared, but he didn't say anything. We moved through the tunnels in silence. It does that to people. You're always listening. We could hear sounds echoing in the distance all around us. They were just sounds that the tunnels make. It was easy to hear voices in the tunnels. It would be easy to go crazy down there.

Jimmy was not there in the room where I left him. I almost went out of my mind. We searched like crazy for him through the tunnels, but he was gone. At first I thought of what Copernik had said, that people disappear all the time down here.

I ran along one of the tunnels until I nearly reached the old abandoned station and then I saw him. Jimmy was on his stomach, to the side of one of the tunnels, looking somewhere ahead. I rushed up to him. He was almost gone. I barely recognized him. It was like there was no blood left in him.

He saw me and there was a brief instant when he looked disappointed, and I know he left so I couldn't find him, to protect me. Then he smiled. Like nothing had happened, like we were just waking up together in the apartment as usual. Jimmy was always like that, even now when he was dying, like it was just another day. He could never be serious for too long.

"Why did you come back?" he asked, and he smiled again. "I thought I was finally rid of you." His voice was so weak.

I told him I was sorry. I told him that we could surrender, at least be alive together, but I knew that he had already decided. They wouldn't let us live. They wouldn't let us leave these tunnels. Not together. He was gone and he knew it. He only wanted to try and protect me now.

The Intern looked at him and I saw from his face that there was nothing left to do. Jimmy already knew. We were just catching up to him.

"They'll be here, Ann," Jimmy said. "Go."

I think it was the first time since we had started all this that he called me by my name. I don't even think Jimmy saw the Intern. I don't think he knew he was there. He only saw me. It was all that mattered.

I opened the bag and started to take out some bandages. It seemed so little. My friend put his hand on my shoulder. This time I turned to look at him. He was trying to tell me what I already knew. We left Jimmy and walked a little way, far enough so that Jimmy couldn't hear us.

My friend told me he was sorry and gave me some more pills. Painkillers. He told me these were stronger than the others. I thanked him and asked if he could find his way back on his own. He said he could. I didn't believe him. I could see that he was unsure, afraid. I forgot just how confusing it was being down there, even if you knew the tunnels fairly well.

I got him to a spot where I knew he could make it back on his own. Once more he said he was sorry. He asked that I go with him, said that there was nothing more to be done for Jimmy, except to try and make him as comfortable as possible.

We could tell them where he was and they could go down for him later.

I told him that I wanted to stay with Jimmy. He said he was worried that I would be caught if I stayed down there. He said I could go back and give Jimmy all the pills, just let him go to sleep. Find peace.

He said I still had a chance to get away. He still had some contact with the old group, he might be able to get help, enough at least to get me out of the city. I'm ashamed to admit that I was tempted, I almost went back with him. I was that close. Instead I took those pills from him and thanked him again. He saw that I meant it.

I asked him how much longer. He said an hour at most. Probably less. There were sounds again in the tunnels behind us. I couldn't be sure if they were real. I said that he better go.

Before he left I thanked him again. I told him that his wife seemed nice. All the bullshit that polite people say to each other. It didn't mean a thing anymore.

When I got back I told Jimmy we had to try and make it back to the room. I knew it was impossible when I was saying it. I just wasn't ready to give up completely. I didn't want him to know how serious it was, how hopeless it was. But he knew. He didn't want to play the game anymore.

He caressed my face again.

"Why did you return?" he asked me. I couldn't help the tears then. Why did he think? I felt bad about what I was thinking just a few minutes before. How close I had come to going back without him.

"Was it worth it?" he said.

He was pleading with me, I could see it in his eyes. He wanted to know if any of it was worth it. He wanted compassion. I knew it was all he had left.

"Yes," I said, and at that moment I didn't believe any of it. I didn't tell him that I would get that bastard Copernik, and Vecchio, or anything like that. I just wanted to be gone from there. Jimmy knew it too.

"It's alright," he told me. "I failed you, Ann. I'm so sorry. I want you to go. Maybe he can help you."

So he knew my friend had been there.

I ignored him and started to apply the bandages, but my hands were shaking, I fumbled everything. It was pathetic. He took my hands and moved them away. The tampons fell out of the bag.

"Shit," he said and started to laugh. It was then, when I heard him laugh, that I knew it was really over. I was angry at his laughter, at his suggestion that I would go with anybody but him, angry that he knew I was thinking about it.

"Please, Jimmy. There's a hospital. It's close. Real close."

It sounded so ridiculous. We both knew he would never make it. There was nothing more to say about it. I just couldn't arrive at the same place. Not yet.

"We can still leave the city. We can try something else later. We just have to leave the city."

He smiled again. I was furious at him, at that smile. He was still testing my loyalty and my love. Even now. He was still asking if it was worth it. This time I wasn't going to back down.

"Let me stay with you, Jimmy."

"No. I want you to live, Ann. I should've listened to you."

"But that's not what we talked about." How hollow my words sounded. I could've been reading from a script.

"Things change. You have a chance. Take it."

To my shame I was silent. Truth is I wanted to live. I wanted to go on, in some way, any way. With or without him.

"Leave, baby. Please. Please."

This time I saw that it was really what he wanted. This time I saw that he knew it was also what I wanted.

I told him about the pills.

And then he nodded and I kissed him and left. I knew that if I didn't leave right then, I might never leave. There were no tears, no profound last words to each other. Coward that I am, I was angry at his stubbornness, at his selfishness, at his courage, at his willingness to let me go, to recognize the coward that I am. I left, and when I looked back for the last time, he had already turned away from me, waiting. I left. This time there was no going back.

I walked like I was already dead. I watched my legs moving forward, following muscle memory again. I couldn't even be sure where I was going. I left that to my legs. I let them lead me wherever they wanted to take me. It didn't matter anymore. Even after everything Jimmy said, even after what he said he wanted, I thought I could see disappointment in his eyes at the end.

That was the last time I talked to Jimmy. As I left I could see above him the painting of the worker at the station. He was just as concerned with that hammer, just as unaware of what was happening around him, like he had been down there way too long. Jimmy looked so tiny beneath him. It was only a few minutes until I heard the first shots. I stopped and listened. There was no question of me going back. I felt ashamed for what I had been thinking only a few minutes before. I just wanted it to be quick. It was silent for a few seconds and I hoped that it was over but then I heard shouting and automatic fire. It went on a few seconds more and then it was quiet again. Please let it be over, I thought.

I waited in agony for a few minutes. Then it was quiet again.

I continued along the tunnel. I don't know what I felt then. Ashamed. Scared.

When I reached the vent and was about to turn the corner, I looked back. Jimmy was a long way off, still lying on his stomach facing away from me, watching the tunnel. I called out to him and I thought he turned for a moment slightly and smiled again and nodded then went back to watching the tunnel. Maybe I imagined it. I don't think he heard me. I think he was already dead. His head was down. He was so still. He had his arm and gun propped up on his jacket. No, it was that stillness, the kind that meant you weren't going to move again.

Kaz's map showed a utility door not far ahead. When I got there it had been braced across with metal strips. It was impossible to open. They were doing it to all the exits now.

The door to the vent was barred. It was useless. I could hear someone shouting, not Jimmy, and then gunshots for some time and I froze and then there were a few more, and then it stopped.

I had to see. I went back a little. I could see Copernik lift Jimmy's head up by the hair and stare at his face. There were three other policemen there. The little man in the suit was standing nearby, away from Copernik. I could see a gun in his hand. I had seen two of them before, that time in Queens, outside the apartment. They were all in it together. All of them. Big surprise.

They stood around Jimmy like he was some animal they had just hunted down. I saw Copernik smile and say something to Jimmy. But I was sure Jimmy was already dead. I aimed my gun at the fat prick but I couldn't shoot. I was too afraid. If I could have been numb, no feeling, if it had been even an hour before, I could have done it. But I was scared of dying on that fucking roller coaster again. I wanted to live. Jimmy knew it all along. It was all bullshit for me. I knew that now. I hated myself for it. I knew that Jimmy didn't care if I believed or not. He just wanted me to live, fake and coward that I am.

I could see one of them pick up the little container of pills and hand them to Copernik. Jimmy had probably never taken any of them. He wanted to be awake as long as possible to try and help me get away. I have to believe that.

A policeman said something to Copernik, who turned viciously and pointed his gun at him. He was in charge, no mistake about it. Then they both looked in my direction. They saw me. The man in the suit shouted something to me, but I couldn't understand. I turned and ran.

They were moving towards me. When I got to the door of the vent again I had forgotten that it was barred. So that was it. So stupid I almost laughed. I couldn't move. I didn't care at that moment. It was over. I got my gun ready and waited. We would at least all go out like revolutionaries. That had to be worth something. I was ready now. Maybe I had always been ready and just didn't know it.

Funny how you can change like that in an instant. When you know it's done. When it's done and you know it. You just know.

You look around and there's nowhere to go. Game over. There's almost a relief, you get calm and quiet. It takes something to get to that point, to resign to death. It's a kind of relief that you don't have to worry about your little life anymore. Once there is no other choice. All exits gone. You live your whole life looking for exits, for escape routes, always moving towards that final exit, the one you don't come back from.

Jimmy once told me he had read a poem somewhere about death, and there was a part that said that when death comes, it also brings peace. You'll come out the other side. No matter how much pain you're in, it'll end, it always ends, and you'll come out the other side. I thought of that now. I was so calm with those words. I never knew words could do that, make you feel that way. Bottom line, there would at least be peace at the other end of this.

I wouldn't be taken alive. That peace had to come quickly for me, not through a haze of pain and fear. I would at least try and take Copernik out before that happened.

I waited. I had two magazines of ammunition left. I decided I would start firing as soon as I saw them. The longer I waited the less I was sure. If I surrendered, maybe they wouldn't kill me. I could cut some sort of deal. I would be alive. I could still see my family.

I could hear them now, coming towards me through the tunnels. They were coming in both directions. They were making so much noise. I had become used to moving quietly down here. They were as loud as elephants in those tunnels.

I heard Copernik's voice. He was in the group ahead coming right at me. They were close. When I heard that voice I knew it was hopeless. There was so much cruelty in that voice. I crouched, raised my gun towards that group and waited. I would try and get Copernik, although I knew at that distance it was hopeless. It would take a miracle. My arms were shaking so much I had to lower them. What was taking them so long? There was sweat in my eyes. I had trouble seeing. It was so hot down there, why was it so hot?

Then I saw the first of the group. It was no surprise that Copernik wasn't in the lead. Where was that fucking coward?

Then I saw her. The young girl. I wasn't sure she was real. She came out of nowhere and led me by the arm. No, I wasn't sure she was real. She led me to a door that we had never seen before. I went through it. When I turned around again she was gone. She didn't say one word to me.

I soon found out where it led. It was familiar. When I reached the grate at the Chinese restaurant on East 34th I waited, watching the diners and crying as silently as possible. It all seemed so quiet and lovely. I was so hungry. I couldn't look at the food. No one followed me. I hoped the little girl was safe.

A young girl sitting with her parents in the restaurant heard me and looked towards the grate. I think she saw me because she smiled and I was afraid she would tell her parents but she turned away again. I moved back a little and when she looked at the grate again she wouldn't see me. She soon lost interest. Her smile made me cry even more. I slept. I was so tired.

When the dining room finally emptied that night I was able to twist my body around and kick the grate. It took me four tries but Kaz was right, it was rusted enough. Maybe I'm wrong but when Kaz told me that, about the grate, maybe he knew something would happen and that I would need it. I don't know. I have to believe there's something to it. The grate made a huge crash on the floor and I crawled out. I could barely straighten my body. Two restaurant employees came in but said nothing. They let me walk past them. Maybe they thought it was too weird to say anything. Maybe I just walked through their blind spot. Maybe Jimmy was looking after me.

I walked through the restaurant to the street. I was covered with dirt, my clothes were torn, my hand bleeding. A real mess. I walked through that restaurant crying, dead, explosives and gun in my hands and no one stopped me. Maybe Jimmy was right after all. The more blatant you are, the more they are willing to disbelieve what's in front of them. You create your own blind spot. Like some kind of hypnosis. A lot of good that did us.

I can't remember much more about that day. I don't know if they followed me out of the restaurant. I remember walking, dazed, along the streets, at night, a long time before I went into a hotel, entering the lobby restroom, getting cleaned up as much as I could. I must have asked for a room because the next thing I remember was waking up on the bed and it was night and I could hear the traffic and I thought I can't go back into the tunnels again. I was through with that. They could find me and shoot me right then and there. I wasn't going back down there.

Just one more time. It turned out to be a few more than that.

I never made another attempt to contact my friend the Intern. It was too risky for him and his family. He had done and risked enough already. Leave him alone. Let him go on with his life.

I brought up some of the explosives the police couldn't find, including that weird plywood contraption Kaz had made. I brought them in a shopping bag, right into the hotel. No one stopped me, no one recognized me, and if they did, what would I be doing walking around like this, like anyone else? No, it had to be someone else. In a city this big, there would always be hundreds of people who looked just like me.

The hatred helped me. Before I could get to Copernik I had to tie up some more loose ends. Two days later, in the early morning, I bombed the headquarters of my friend's radical group, near the Port Authority. I made sure no one was inside. Now they would know fear. I wanted someone else to know fear.

After that I lay in wait for my friend for two nights outside her apartment building. I had my gun ready. On the second night I saw her returning alone, talking on her cellphone, probably still spinning shit about the right-wing hit on their headquarters. I walked up behind her. She never saw me. I raised the gun and she turned around and looked right at me and stopped talking.

I came close, so close. That look of being lost, of desperation and helplessness, maybe that would be enough. I don't know.

I wanted to see it on someone else's face. Or maybe I just wanted to fuck her up. I never got any of it. She just waited, like it was inevitable, like that insurance doctor that other time. Suspended in space and time. Do it and get it over with. I couldn't do it. I lowered my gun and turned and walked away.

She never said anything, never yelled anything out. There were no more lectures. Something smacked the pavement hard near me and then something else whizzed by my head. I turned back and she had her arms raised towards me. Even from that distance I recognized the Walther pistol in her hand. Jimmy had taught us well about guns. She had the stance, everything, like she had studied from the same fucking FBI manual.

So much for her peace movement. I ran behind one of the nearby buildings and when I peeked back she was still coming at me. Just like she was supposed to. Just like the manual said. Be relentless.

I jammed my gun into my coat pocket and ran along the building. There was little traffic. Few people walking around at that hour. I didn't know what to think. Was she just pissed at me, did she suspect I bombed the center, was she trying to get the reward, become a hero? Maybe she was working for the FBI all along, maybe it was all a trap. Anything was possible, nothing made sense to me anymore, only survival, the chance to live and try and make sense of it later, the chance to mull it through over a cold beer and some fries.

She kept walking and firing, scattering people. A woman was hit and cried out. People were on their cellphones now, calling the police. I kept running, past the restaurant where we met the other night, past a park, until I got tired and didn't give a shit anymore. There were no more buildings to duck into, no alleys, no subway stations. Fuck it.

She was still coming right at me, her arms raised. I took my gun out and started walking back towards her. I hated her, I wanted her dead. I could hear the bullets whizzing by, hitting the building next to me. Not one hit me. She cried out then crumpled on the sidewalk. She raised her gun again and fired but it wasn't even close. She was trying to get another clip in when I came up to her. I told her to stop but she kept fumbling with the clip, having trouble getting it set. Not enough manual training maybe.

I wrestled the gun away from her. She had been hit in the leg, below the knee, probably a ricochet from the pavement. I was all ready to shout at her, yell at her that she was a crazy, radical piece of shit, to hit her, but I never got the chance.

"You killed him!" she screamed at me. "You killed him!"

I was stunned by those words. I thought she was hysterical, maybe because of the gunshot wound. She was always a little weird in college, flipping from passive to aggressive in a second. I asked her what the fuck she was talking about. I just wanted her to shut up.

"My brother. You killed him!" She was crying now.

I didn't say anything. Something cold gripped my body. I was paralyzed. I knew right away what it was all about. But it was impossible. A trick.

"He was inside," she said. I could barely understand her now, she was so hysterical.

"There was no one inside," I answered. My voice was sounding detached again, on autopilot. Insincere. "There were no lights on." This was madness. I had to protect myself from these strange ideas. Don't let her get into my head. Who could I trust anymore?

"No, he was in there. Sometimes he just sits there and thinks. In the dark. He's always done that, since we were kids. He was in there!"

What was she talking about? I had to sit down. My legs were buckling under me. I couldn't think. I didn't even know where we were. Some city lights, some traffic up and down the street. Some people standing around us, others walking past, staring. I knew what she was saying was true. It had to be.

And then I heard someone say they were sorry. Was it me? Maybe. And then I saw my friend speaking to me. It was her. She was crying and saying that she was sorry. That it was the same person that I met at the restaurant the other night. Her brother, not her boyfriend. That her brother wanted to help me after she had told him, at the restaurant, but I didn't come back. I was too afraid. He had wanted to help Jimmy and me. And she was sorry now that she wouldn't let him.

Here she was, apologizing to me. The only person I ever hurt was someone kind, someone who wanted to change The System, make a difference, just like me. Her brother. A friend. A complete innocent. I killed him.

I thought I heard police sirens somewhere, I wasn't sure. I got up and started walking. Someone reached out for me and I raised my gun and they left me alone. They all left me alone. My legs were carrying me again, somewhere, anywhere. I had to get off the street, away from there. I looked at my left hand and saw the Walther and dropped it into a recycling bin. I put my own gun back into my coat pocket and had only one thought, to get off the street.

In my mind I saw her brother again. He was coming out of the restaurant, shy, his hands jammed into his olive green military jacket. His thick black curly hair. He was so good-looking and kind. So kind and understanding. Dedicated to the cause, to the lives of others. Someone fighting The System, and not killed by The System. Killed by me. It was all I could do not to laugh. It must be some fucking cosmic joke.

Muscle memory took me back into the parking garage and through the maintenance door into the tunnels again. I had become something now that couldn't live above or below. Something that could only find safety and peace now in darkness down there. I had become worse than the rats and other creatures who lived down here. Hiding from everything. Doing everything necessary to survive. Anything.

I stayed in the tunnels for almost a day, full of remorse and grief. I wanted to see my family. To touch them. To be in my mother's arms. To ask forgiveness from her, from my brother, from everything, for everything I had done. I walked around. All through the tunnels. I needed to find Jimmy, be with him. I never found him.

The next day I was afraid to go up again. The whole city would be watching. Finally I went back to the hotel and slept again. I didn't want to be clean. Not yet. I didn't deserve it.

I couldn't look at TV or the papers. I knew what I would find there. I didn't care anymore. I only had one thing on my mind. I fell asleep again.

A few days later I saw Copernik on television. So fucking pleased with himself. He was telling everyone how brave Belden had been, how he deserved an award for valor. They showed some strange faces on TV and in the papers. Faces of Muslim terrorists whose bodies were found in the subway where they had been killed by police. They were the same people I had seen in those cocoon bags.

There was nothing on the bombing of the headquarters of the radicals. Nothing about the brother. It was Copernik and the New York police who had the floor. Even the FBI was not around.

Of course there was no mention of Jimmy or Kaz. I never found out what became of their bodies. They were probably somewhere in the tunnels, maybe in that abandoned elevator shaft. I looked around the tunnels as much as I could risk during those days. There were still police moving around down there.

No, they were not looking for any other suspects, at least none that they mentioned. But I knew Copernik and the others were looking for me. Copernik said that no one would believe me, about him, Belden, the man in the suit, the other police, anything. But I knew he was still worried. He wouldn't be calm until I disappeared for good.

God how good a hot shower felt! I'm ashamed to say that it was almost all I could think of those last days. I wanted to forget everything that had happened. I tried. But I couldn't.

I remembered hearing Copernik talking to Belden in the tunnels, saying that they would have to go back to their precinct. I knew that was their station. Midtown South.

I left the hotel that night. The next day I took a cab and checked into another hotel a few blocks from the Midtown South Precinct Police Station on West 35th and 8th. I stayed there for three days, watching the squat police station building and wondering if I had the courage to go ahead with what I was going to do. I thought about it a long time. I was scared. I could just leave the city. No problem. I felt I could go anywhere I wanted now. I wrestled with it day and night.

From my window I could see the police coming and going. There were still some media people and cameras there, but it had calmed down a lot. It wasn't long before I saw Copernik come out and talk to the media. Not long after the reporters were gone I saw someone else come out of the station alone and then quickly leave in a car. It was our old friend Vecchio. I looked for patterns, I looked for a system in their movements.

After a few days I had it. Every day at 12:30 p.m. Copernik left, sometimes by himself, sometimes with others, always in his car. The car would always stop at the stop sign for a moment then head along 8th and out of sight. Every day, without fail. Copernik was a man of strict habits. A man without fear, a man confident enough not to change those habits. That was his little system. It made him strong, and it made him vulnerable.

One day I took a chance. I used one of the fake IDs to rent a car. I held my breath but nothing triggered any alarms at the rental agency. I waited outside the police station and sure enough I saw Copernik and another policeman pull onto 8th and pass me. I stayed back far enough, terrified I would be seen. Back far enough that I lost them in the traffic. I drove faster and went past the car, almost missing it. There it was, parked on the street in a no parking zone, right in front of the same restaurant where our world had collapsed only a week ago. In the same spot where Copernik and Belden had parked that time.

I had forgotten just how close it was to the police station. I parked up the street, got out and walked back towards the restaurant. Someone came out of the restaurant and I turned around and made like I was window shopping. It was Vecchio, having a cigarette. I stood there for some time. I could feel Vecchio's eyes on me. Then I went back up the street, passed my rental car and turned the corner. It was some time before I got enough courage to look again. Vecchio had gone back in.

No, it was even riskier here than at the station. They were confident, so fucking confident here, but also cautious and alert. Maybe they felt exposed here, animals outside the safety of their dens. I had to be careful. There could be people watching. I got into the rental car and drove back. In front of the rental agency there was an unmarked car and a police car sitting up the street.

Maybe alarms did go off after all. I drove past the agency, made sure I wasn't being followed then pulled into a parking garage, paid for a spot, then left the car, tossing the keys into the trash, and went back to the hotel.

Next day I got the transit schedule from the hotel, and caught a bus at 12:30 going along 8th. We reached the restaurant in a quarter hour and there was Copernik's car. Same spot.

I remembered Kaz's surprise when he entered the restaurant and saw Copernik and me. Who had suggested we go to that restaurant? Kaz I think, but I couldn't be sure.

No, it had to be Vecchio who had set us up. I don't know what Vecchio told Kaz, the reason we should be at that restaurant at that time. I never found out. But Kaz was as innocent as we were. As stupid and trusting as we were. I had to believe that. Kaz would never have betrayed us. Not on purpose.

That night in the hotel I went over everything. A new fear came over me, something much worse. It was always going to be a losing game, right? The System was all-knowing, it was everywhere, it had been ahead of us all along, even before we went under the city. It had always wanted us to do exactly what we were doing. And it made sure we were always going to do it. How can you fight something that's already inside you? That has already made you a part of it?

I couldn't be sure of anything I did anymore. I was paralyzed again. I wasn't even sure Jimmy wasn't involved. Maybe he had planned it with Kaz and Vecchio and Copernik all along and then was betrayed by one of them. I had all kinds of crazy thoughts. Everything I was doing seemed rehearsed, done before, planned by someone else. Anything was possible.

I watched for days. I wouldn't allow myself to be frozen. I had to get out, find some answers. I even went over to the station, twice, to see for myself. No disguises, just me. I went into our bank and took some money out. No one questioned me about anything. I didn't exist anymore. I was beginning to like not existing. There was a sense of power that went with it.

I tested Jimmy's theory many times over those days. I owed him that much. Copernik walked almost right past me once. Alright, I did turn away from him, I mean there's only so much of a chance you can take. But I bet it could have worked. Copernik was in the spotlight now. Everybody was his friend. He had no enemies. His guard was as down as it would ever get. No, I would be out of the city by now. Long gone. He knew a coward when he saw one. Just like Jimmy saw it in me.

Nobody recognized me. Nobody cared. I was in their blind spot. They were too busy spinning their terrorist theories to the media and the other cops. They loved it. I didn't know the police were such a vain bunch of assholes. There couldn't have been only a few terrorists involved to do what they had done. There must have been a large cell and organization behind it. No one else could have pulled this off. Muslim citizens were being questioned, brought into the station, into FBI headquarters. It was only a matter of time until Copernik headed his own anti-terrorist group.

Only Muslims or fanatic sympathizers could have that kind of clout. I don't know if it was all bullshit but the media had computer communications outages all through the city the next day, when I finally took out the weird building's communications room under Lexington Avenue. Maybe Kaz had been right all along about his mythic nexus building. Maybe it was all connected. He did a good enough job teaching me about explosives. And I added some of my own twists in the next few days. I was adding fuel to the fire, as much as I could.

One day I saw the little guy in the suit coming out of the station. He had probably talked to Copernik about the blast. The little FBI prick looked like he would have nine lives. They were all in it together. All of them.

I never hated The System more than at that moment. They were all so busy moving around, little drones, doing their little part to keep The System fucking everybody. So loyal, like they had invented everything around them.

Proud parents of the status quo. They couldn't think of anything else, anything different from what they had before them, couldn't imagine anything different from what already was, and is, like they had been doing this for a thousand years.

Yeah, proud guardians of everything around them. Don't think, don't question, keep inside the lines and destroy anything that even remotely walks funny and looks like a threat to their precious here and now. And how easily they kill. We should have taken more of it down. I had a taste for blood again.

There was never any mention of us. Nobody wanted to know that three young kids from Brooklyn could do this. No, there was something else at work here. No photos. No, this was too important and big to wrap it around three friends in their twenties, three disaffected suburban kids who saluted the flag and cared about baseball and getting laid, like any ordinary American kids.

It had to be bigger. They would use it to create a conspiracy of massive proportions that they could use to scare the shit out of everyone. I don't know how many other people would disappear. They would be preparing more bodies, some poor innocent Muslim types, conspirators that they had killed just in time, while the hunt goes on for the others.

There would always be others. I couldn't believe that it was just Copernik and some of the other police. No doubt the little FBI prick was involved, maybe others in the FBI, maybe it went up all the way, to where? Maybe we could never find out.

I didn't care. I just wanted one of them. And Vecchio. Before what was left of the courage I had was gone for good.

I couldn't sleep anymore. I couldn't think about what they were doing with Jimmy and Kaz's families. Maybe nothing. Maybe the families hadn't even been told. Better that way. Jimmy and Kaz would just disappear, like those drug dealers in the tunnels. Sometimes it's better not to know.

I wondered about my family. Would they be terrorizing my mother and little brother? There was nothing I could do.

I thought of going around to see them, maybe catching my mother alone somehow.

The next day I took a bus out to the suburbs and got off a few miles away from my house and walked the rest of the way.

The police were there. Two cars at either end of the block. What did Copernik tell them about me? Whatever it was, they weren't going to take me in. I wouldn't make it to the station. They were all involved. I had to believe they were.

I waited awhile and then I saw her come out of the house. I don't know what made her do it, but she came out the front door like she wanted to look at one of the plants on the front porch, then she looked up at one of the police cars and then back and straight at me.

We made eye contact. I was so surprised that I almost walked out to the road, in front of the police. I had to know for sure that she saw me. I had to know. She looked so sick and worried, so thin, so much older. She didn't smile, I wanted her so much to smile, just one little connection with the past, but she didn't and I knew then. I would never see her or my little brother again. She knew everything. I had stopped existing.

It was only for a second or two then she flicked her hand as a signal and went inside again. She had always done that, just a little flick of her right wrist as a warning. It had been our secret since I was a kid. I stood there for some time, looking at the windows to see if she and my brother were there, but I never saw them again.

What would my mother say about me? Maybe nothing. Maybe she would forget I had ever been there. I wouldn't blame her.

A police car drove by and I left.

The next day I went into the tunnels for the last time. There were no police there. I found the girl again. She told me what had happened. They took away Jimmy and Kaz and buried them quickly near one of the abandoned stations below 58th Street. She took me to see where they lay, side by side, by an old track rail. You only knew by the shallow mounds that anything was there. You had to be looking for them.

The girl had placed little plastic flowers on the graves. She told me the one on the right was Jimmy's grave. That he was sleeping there.

We stayed there for some time. There was nothing I could do to bring them back into the daylight. It was OK. There was peace down here.

They had rounded up some of the mole people, after the shootings. They had thrown two of them, including the older man, into one of the old elevator shafts.

They believed the other mole people knew where I was, but only the girl did. And they never found her. None of the others down there gave her up, even though the police said there was a reward for information about me. Two of them were rewarded by being tossed into the shaft.

The girl described one of the policemen. The one with the voice like a dog barking, she said. Copernik.

After that, the others had scattered to all parts of the tunnels. The police and some other strangely dressed men had entered the tunnels again and had been looking around for a few days. There were other police with them. Probably FBI. Copernik was with them again. He was giving the FBI a tour of the tunnels, explaining what had happened, where the other terrorists could be hiding. He was the big hero now. Even the feds were listening to him.

They had brought workmen down there with tools and supplies and had blocked more of the exit and entrance points, but there were so many others that it made little difference. There would always be a way out. The danger was turning a corner and suddenly running into them.

The girl said the FBI even brought dogs into the tunnels, and they set up cameras at different points, like those animal trackers on TV. The dogs hated it down there. At a certain point they refused to go any further into the tunnels. Who knows what they smelled and heard down there. It didn't matter. The police and the feds knew what I looked like. The cameras might record me. So what? I didn't care. They were easy to spot anyway. I just didn't want the girl to get into trouble.

I was extra careful not to be seen with her when we were near the cameras. She was precious to me. She was the only thing I had left.

I was tired of the darkness. I would never go down again, I promised myself. I asked the girl if she wanted me to come back and take her out of the tunnels, but she said no, and I believed her. I realized she was just as afraid of the city as I was of what was beneath it. I realized that she, of all people, was at least free of The System, that thing that was at work above the tunnels, that thing that couldn't reach or touch her. That thing that had crushed Jimmy, Kaz and me.

I needed to do one more thing, and I hoped I would be given enough time. I would be out there, in the open. I would live in that blind spot for as long as I could, and then run towards the lion's den one more time.

I stayed down there for three days. I brought the girl more clothes, including a new jacket and some pants. It was starting to get colder in the tunnels. Or maybe it was me. I was cold a lot those last days. I showed her where all the remaining medicine and food was. She could take it to the others. It would at least get some use.

She watched me with curiosity as I made some changes to the last bomb. My movements were strange, detached, like my hands weren't part of me anymore. There was some memory driving them on. I felt nothing. I was something that could vanish at any time. The girl didn't approve but I think she understood. I made her stand some distance away from me. I didn't want her hurt.

I lost some of the instructions from Kaz that I had written down, but I tried my best to remember what went where with this bomb. I couldn't be sure. I prayed for it to go right. Just this once.

We stayed in the room with the warm pipes and the mattress. No one came to look for her, at least no one we could see. It was quiet down there, peaceful. The world had stopped for a short time. It was wonderful.

After three days I had to leave. If I stayed longer I don't think I would be able to leave. I would be there in the tunnels forever. I read books to her, children's books that I had read so long ago. They were as strange to her as the tunnels were to me when I first came down. When was that? God, years ago.

I gave her more medicine for her cold, which was getting worse. She was coughing during the night. I thought the heat and moisture in the room were making her worse, affecting her lungs and breathing. I had to get us out of the tunnels.

Something happened in those days. I held her close, I couldn't let her go, and when we slept the warmth from our bodies entered each other. Just like with me and Jimmy. Suddenly I couldn't imagine life without her. It was always supposed to be this way. No other way was possible.

It wasn't just me. Something was also happening to the girl. On the third day she asked if she could go with me, leave the tunnels. I cried with happiness. Here was my salvation. We would leave the tunnels and start again. Somewhere. Anywhere. I no longer wanted to die. We would live for each other. Nothing else mattered now. Only to live and to be with her. No one would stand in our way. She was my one true cause now.

I thanked the girl when it was time to leave. It sounded so silly but it was true. She had saved my life. She was sorry she could not save the others, Jimmy and Kaz. I loved her.

I was so happy. There had been enough death already. When she asked to go with me I stopped making the bomb, right then and there. I dropped everything. It was no longer important. It seemed strange that it had ever been important. Only saving this life standing in front of me was important. Nothing else mattered. She was giving me another chance.

When it was almost time she asked that I let her go back and say goodbye to the others. I didn't want to let her go but she said it would be alright. She would be waiting for me at the painting of the young woman, at the abandoned station. I could meet her there and then we could leave the tunnels and get to Penn Station and get on a train, leave the city and be on our way.

I dressed the girl in her best clothes and then I left. I was so excited that I could barely find my way out to the city.

My mind was racing ahead to making preparations, leaving the hotel, taking only what I needed, making sure I wasn't followed, going back into the tunnels. I would take the entrance through the parking garage on Madison, it was the safest, there was never anyone around. Then I started to panic because I knew I was over-planning and over-thinking and being too cautious. I thought of Jimmy and the whole thing about thinking like them and being predictable. Maybe they would be waiting, expecting it. I didn't know what to do. I was frozen, scared stiff. Then I started laughing. I was so confused. No, I'd wing it, whatever way in came into my head when I left the hotel, that's the one I would take. It would be the last time, and I would do it like we always did it, like Jimmy wanted it. One last time. Fuck it. Then no more. No more. It's screwed me up enough, I thought.

When I was ready I said goodbye to the girl and went up to the city again. That sense of doom, always there with Jimmy, Kaz and me, soon came back again. It had missed me. It wanted me back. It found me in the city.

I went back down to the tunnels for one more thing. The most foolish of things. I forgot to give the girl the small watch she liked. The first time we met I saw that she admired my cheap watch. I felt then that I needed to get it to her at all costs. It seemed like the most important thing in the world then. I needed to get it to her, to see her face, to hold her one more time before we started our new lives. I needed her strength and reassurance that it was all true, that it was really happening, that the others had not taken her back with them when I was gone.

She was not at the painting. I found her not far from where I had left her the day before. She was lying there, her skull smashed in. She looked so small, like a doll cast to the side. Maybe it was Copernik, maybe one of the others down there who didn't like her because they saw her talking to me, or because she was different from them, because she was wearing new clothes. I don't know. I was lost, out of answers. I sat with her for a long time then buried her beside Jimmy and Kaz, putting my watch on her wrist. It slid to her elbow.

Her arm was so thin. Then I knelt there and cried for a long time. I never felt so alone and helpless. Where did I have to go now? Maybe I could lie there. Fade into the darkness. I was ready to make this place my tomb.

I didn't cry for long. I don't know why. I just stared at her grave like it was all inevitable, the natural play of things. Like fate had always something to do with it.

Then I left. The more I thought about it the more I hated. I remember thinking how good it was to hate again. I was so focused now. Just one thing in front of me. One more thing to do. It was all so simple. Maybe it was always supposed to be.

I was suddenly staring at the man in the suit. He had his gun on me. If I had my gun in my hand I would have used it and he would have killed me. Simple as that. He must have been standing nearby all along. Why did he wait? So that was it, I thought. It was all over. I didn't have any fight left. I just stared at him. If he wanted to kill me right there, he could do it.

His suit was a mess, flaked with mud. You could never really be clean down here. He just started talking, like he had been waiting for this moment all his life to talk.

"It was Copernik," he said, pointing at the little girl's grave. "He killed her." I didn't say anything, didn't move. Maybe it was Copernik, maybe not. What was he waiting for? He seemed to be alone, I didn't see anyone else. The others could have been anywhere. You can hide a tank down there with all those corners, no problem. He was struggling with something. You could see it. I could barely stand. I felt weak and hungry and used up.

"Do you want me to kill him?" I said. I don't know why. It just seemed like the truth. I could sense it was what he wanted. I could almost read his thoughts.

He was silent. Then he nodded.

"And after? What then?" I asked.

Then he talked again and there was no stopping him this time. He told me straight out that Copernik was causing all kinds of trouble in his department, in the FBI, that Copernik's little play for power was about to come to an end, that I would be taken care of by the Bureau, if I did this one thing and removed Copernik. My family would be OK, he'd make sure of it. He'd make sure that Jimmy and Kaz's families could move on with their lives, no harm done, they were innocents as far as he and the Bureau were concerned.

That wouldn't be the case with Copernik. He would make the lives of our families a nightmare. They would never find peace as long as he was around. He was a danger to everyone. Even the FBI.

After it was done, I would go to a building near the police station and there would be protection waiting. They would get me out of the city. Anywhere. I'd be free to go, maybe even eventually get back with my family. The Bureau could do anything. They could make it happen. That's what the man in the suit told me.

If he told me he could move the earth I'd believe him. I knew it was just another power play, The System finding and leveraging another weakness, the same old story. I was just buying some time to live a little longer. I had no more chips in the game, not even bluff.

So we went through the motions, playing the game a little longer, my lying that I would do what he said, his lying that he would do what he said. In two days he would make sure Copernik was at the station. He would make sure Copernik would be leaving the station in his car around 1:30 in the afternoon. After I took care of Copernik I would walk around the corner to a warehouse on 8th avenue. There was an alley on the south side of the warehouse. I could walk along the alley to a blue painted door, and open the door to freedom. Just like a fairy tale. When you wish upon a star. That simple. There would be agents waiting there to take me out of the city.

That simple. Either way, if I died trying to kill Copernik, it was good for the man in the suit. If I lived and killed Copernik, it was also good. Either way I would be dead before I left the city. There was no way they would let me live, either way.

He didn't say another word. They had all been used up, a limited supply. That was OK. He didn't have to say anything more.

I ask you what you would have done. He knew he had me. There was no fight left in me. I was done. I didn't trust him, he didn't trust me, but we acted like trust was the only thing left between us.

I wanted to ask him about the bombing at the radical center. He had to know it was me. Maybe he didn't. Maybe he didn't care, one way or another. No, I wouldn't make it any easier for them. If there was something else going on here, I would play along. I wanted to live, and I didn't care anymore how I could do it.

"Did you know Kaz?" I asked.

He was like stone. He only smiled. Of course he did. He knew all of us, our families, everything. He probably knew the secret of the universe. Maybe The System had lost this one, had let him go. Maybe it was just something personal. It didn't matter to me anymore. The only thing that mattered was that we both wanted Copernik dead. Maybe for different reasons, but dead all the same. Everything the man in the suit had just told me, it was all about Copernik. That was all I really heard and understood.

"You saw us that time, didn't you?" I said. "You saw us in that room with the heating pipes."

He told me that he had seen us.

This time it was my turn with the words. I asked him why he didn't call the others. Why he just walked away, although I knew it was because something else was in play here.

"Does it matter now?" he said.

"What about my family?" I asked again. "Will they be alright? Please tell me they will be."

He answered that they would be alright, that they were not part of any of this.

I think I believed him. I wasn't sure. I just had to hear it from him again, as though the truth was tied to the number of times something was said. I had had enough. No more games. No more guessing. He could shoot me or take me in. His choice.

"Did you kill Jimmy?" I asked.

He said Jimmy was already dead when they reached him. I didn't know what to believe.

I turned around and started walking away. I never answered his offer one way or the other.

"Do you believe in it?" he asked.

I knew what he meant but I didn't answer. I could hear the frustration in his voice. What did this man believe in? I didn't know, God, The System, the Yankees, cold fusion, maybe nothing at all. Maybe he was just as at home and just as lost in these tunnels, these shadows, as I was. I hoped that he was.

I didn't turn around. I was suddenly full of hatred again. I hated my helplessness, my own survival. I just shook my head and continued walking.

I thought I heard him say my name, I thought I heard him say goodbye. I wasn't sure.

I closed my eyes waiting for the bullet to hit. Just like hanging suspended over the elevator shaft, don't look, close your eyes, it'll be over in a second or two. Time is your friend. I wanted to ask him why. I wanted to know, to demand to know. I wanted him to answer me. I wanted him to tell me who he was. When I turned around again he was gone.

I swore I would never go back in those tunnels again. This time I really meant it. No matter what. There was no peace down here anymore, only death and the past. I could see my mother reading about my death. No, most likely I would wind up like Jimmy and Kaz. Just gone. Like we were never there. Faded into the darkness.

In the hotel room I prepared the final part of the plan. Got everything ready. I didn't sleep at all. My mind was up to its old cruel routine, telling me to sleep and then waking me up just before sleep came, over and over again. I couldn't decide, I knew I wouldn't decide until the second I had to leave. There were no unmarked cars on the street outside the hotel, at least none that I could see, but that didn't mean anything. No, they were certainly out there somewhere. Truth is they could kill me any time they wanted. I wasn't sure they would wait first to see if I would really do it. Maybe I had a little more rope to play with. It was all up to the man in the suit now.

I wasn't sure what or who would be waiting for me. A friend, an enemy? Maybe both. I didn't know who the players were anymore. Everyone was playing their part. I didn't know what mine was. I wasn't even sure who I was working for anymore, me or the other side. Maybe there was never any difference. Killing Copernik was the only thing that made sense. Nothing else.

Would they let me go? Just slip out the back of the hotel and disappear. I had all kinds of wild ideas. The night breeds them, doesn't it? I could go see my mom and brother, maybe get close enough to touch them. Then make a run for it, disappear into those quiet streets in Queens. Find my way out. No harm done. Was that illogical? Would they be looking for it? Had they been looking for it all along? They seemed to be ahead of me, waiting for me to arrive, no matter what I did.

I could run through the city, just take a cab and leave. See my family later. It could work.

I could turn myself in. The System could protect me, from Copernik, from the others. The little man in the suit. He would protect me. I had to trust at some point. I had to trust. I couldn't reach that point yet. I knew I never would.

The next day I left the hotel early and joined the hundreds of people on the sidewalk who were getting to work. I stopped and had breakfast in a coffee shop. I was so nervous and shaking so much that my hand was rattling the coffee cup. I didn't think I could go through with it. Not alone. I was so alone. I was thinking about running again. I couldn't breathe. I had to get out.

I left the coffee shop and walked. No, I didn't think I could go through with it. No one was following me. Not that I could see. Maybe he had let me go, the little man in the suit. I just walked, until I was exhausted. It was beautiful, being able to walk in the air, with people all around me. They looked happy enough. I envied them then. They were freer than I was.

There was no one around to rescue me. I was outside everything now, a walking ghost. I didn't exist, I was invisible.

I kept walking. They all looked so much more alive than I did. How could that be? They were all supposed to be dead, walking in that system of deception, and I was supposed to be the one with the vision, the answers. It had all turned around. I was jealous of all of them.

And then I found myself at the corner of 35th and 8th. I didn't stop. I knew if I stopped it would be over. I just had to keep moving.

I saw the warehouse on 8th. An old red brick building like the man in the suit said. I walked up to it. It seemed empty, there was no sound coming from inside, no cars and no truck around. I looked down the alley beside the building and walked down it. The alley was clean, no debris. There was the blue metal door. I tried to open it but it was locked. The whole alley looked like it was scrubbed, unnatural, waiting for something. Maybe me.

I turned back, and walked into the Midtown precinct station at 12:30 p.m.

I saw Copernik and the man with the suit go into one of the back rooms and they came out with Vecchio. The man in the suit looked at me for a second then looked away, like I wasn't there. Did he nod to me, did I imagine that? No, I was on my own. I was always on my own. Our old friend Vecchio turned towards me once, and this time it was my turn to look away. No, it couldn't be me there, I'm sure he was thinking. But I was afraid he recognized me. I waited, so scared, but no one in the station approached me. Who would think that I would walk right into the station?

I walked out again. No, I couldn't do it. Not yet. That night I got everything ready again. There was no sleep again that night. I didn't know what I would do until the morning came. I kept seeing Jimmy's eyes, the eyes of my mother. The pain and disappointment in them.

That night I saw unmarked cars parked on the street outside the hotel. This time they were watching me, waiting. It was like a performance. And the audience was getting restless. The actress hadn't shown yet. Maybe she never would.

Morning came. Friday. I hoped I had enough nerve to go through with it. Fear was waiting for me again. It was always there now. At 1:30 p.m. I was outside the station. I didn't hide. I was through with that. They had to be on time. I didn't know how much longer I could wait.

Finally I saw the three of them leave through the back of the station. I walked over to one of the trash bins and took out the paper bag with Kaz's plywood and bomb. I waited right there with the package. No one stopped me, no one even noticed.

There's that stop sign before you turn onto 35th coming out of the station. That's where I waited. In a few minutes the car appeared. There was a lot of traffic on 8th. They could be waiting there for some time. I left the package on the street and walked away. The car pulled up and stopped, right over the package. I could see Copernik in the driver's seat. Vecchio was not in the car. That prick had nine lives. No man in the suit either. Just Copernik. That was OK. That would do for now.

Two police cars pulled into the station parking lot. One of the officers looked closely at me as they passed me. You could see he was trying to add it together, trying to get the letters to click and tumble, trying to come up with an answer.

Another police car pulled out of the station parking lot and started coming towards the exit, right behind Copernik's car. There was more traffic than I ever saw those days watching the station. A regular freeway now.

I turned for a moment and I know Copernik saw me. I don't know what he could have been thinking at that time. He must have wondered what I was doing there. Maybe at that second he knew what was coming. Maybe we resign ourselves to things faster than we think. We don't even know it. It's just a matter of catching up to it.

I tried to detonate the package with the cellphone but nothing happened. Maybe Kaz was fucking with me one last time. Copernik hit the accelerator and the bomb went off and the back of the car disintegrated.

You know the rest.

6
CHICAGO

The train is picking up speed now. The pain in my shoulder is better. I wish the little girl would come back. I don't know where she is. I need to feel her innocence.

All I know is that we hated this system. And that we felt something better was possible. That's all. We couldn't tell you what that something better was. That wasn't up to us. That was out of our hands.

We're not philosophers or leaders. What could we accomplish? What could we possibly do to make a difference? Nothing. It didn't matter if, by some miracle, we moved The System by one millimeter or by one mile. They could replace this System with another one, and they would, and we wouldn't care. We would have been gone by then.

We never said that what we were doing had a moral reason. We don't know if what we're doing is better for us, for them, for you, for anyone. We don't know what any of this would lead to. A better System? A worse System? Maybe. But it'll always be *a* system, won't it? It'll always protect itself by any means necessary. That's why there's really only one way to go for it. All or nothing.

What did we do, what did we accomplish? I don't know. Like I said a long time ago, sometimes you just have to have faith that there is more to what you're doing than you know. Why you open a certain door, why you turn at a given moment, why you choose one way over another. You know there's something more at work. You feel it. There's no use talking about it.

I don't know who said it, that faith is believing in something you can't see. Maybe there's something to that.

No, Jimmy wouldn't like this kind of thinking. Too soft, too mystical. We can thank The System for that.

No, it's just something that's there, in your gut, something that you know is right and that you have to do, because if you don't try, then you're doomed: they have you and it's a slow death and you'll always wonder and in no time you're starting to form that shell around you, the one that keeps in the guilt and the doubts and the rightness, and before long you don't even know what it was all about, you just sense that something underneath that was always there and that you now hate so much that you'll do anything to forget it, to destroy it, to hate everything and everyone that reminds you of it. It's an embarrassment now, an old friend whom you no longer want to recognize, something that can only remind you of how far you've fallen. You say fuck it.

I have to tell myself this, that it was worth it in some way, that it hasn't been all foolish and tragic. That there was always something worthy. That Jimmy and I should be grateful that we felt what we did, that we tried. That we really tried.

How warm it is now. It feels pleasant. The pain is not so bad. It's hard to write. It's almost done now. No more lies, no more illusions. I only take some comfort in knowing that the police will stop looking for me soon and leave my mother and brother alone. They've already moved on to something else, I'm sure. No one will give a damn about Copernik. And they shouldn't. I hope my family can find some peace. I've caused them so much trouble. I regret that.

The little girl has gone away with her mother. I'm so sad. I fell asleep, I don't know for how long. It's like my entire world is closing around me, with the girl gone. Please don't let me die like this. Please give me something at the end. Something I can take with me.

A young woman has taken their place. She avoids my eyes. She is a reader. She has put me in her blind spot. I deserve it.

It's weird how much she looks like me. As though it was planned. Categorical imperative? Maybe. Maybe it's just my eyes playing tricks. What do we know about these things? It is as though this woman sitting across from me had also reached the point where the path was clear for her. To someone else it's something completely different.

Now the paranoia begins. Is it by chance the woman has chosen her seat in front of me, in this little compartment? There are other seats on the train. I'm sure of it. Have they followed me? No, they would have arrested me already. I relax a little. I still have the gun. In the bag. It has a new magazine. New bullets. I let the bag sit. Fuck it.

She glances at me for a moment but does not smile. She's worried about me. She doesn't know what I'm about. There's no need to worry. I believe we really do understand each other. We just don't know it yet. She puts me back in her blind spot. I'll stay there. No problem.

I try to write a little more, but my fingers feel cold, almost prickly. It can wait.

Finally leaving the city. No more regrets. No, just one more. I wish I was beside them, sleeping there, in the dark, with Jimmy and Kaz and the little girl. It's quiet there. What else would we need? When death comes so does peace, right? I have to believe it. Why did Kaz give me the map of that building on 32nd? Why didn't the police block that door like all the others? I don't know. Maybe there are other things at work that we don't understand. Maybe it's not all on one side. Maybe it evens out sometimes.

I ask you, what would you have done? Tell me, please. Only those who understand will know what I'm asking. What should we have done? What? I don't know. Stayed in The System, been good, played along? Was it so bad, what we tried to do? I'm really confused.

No, it doesn't matter anymore. Fuck it. The end is here. Let it come. It doesn't care about your politics, your beliefs, it doesn't give a shit. I just have to close my eyes. No more system. No more tunnels. No more hate. Please, no more hate.

It doesn't matter anymore. Maybe it never did. Maybe we're nothing but those white numbers and letters that clatter, disappear and reform. Again and again. We only do what we're supposed to do, change how we're supposed to change. Come up with the same answers. Always. And all through this, I just wanted one thing. Jimmy's love. That's all.

Just sleep now.

I wake up again. And again. My mind is fighting me now, having fun with me. Even my own mind won't let me have any peace. Next time I wake up I'm laughing. I can't help myself. I'm thinking of the tampons and Jimmy. I can't help but laugh. Such revolutionaries, we go marching on with our tampons. We never had a chance, did we?

I'm still laughing. What's wrong with me? The woman gets up and leans towards me. I think of reaching for the gun but I hesitate. I've seen her before someplace. I know it. More paranoia. She places a hand on my shoulder. She is only asking me if I'm alright. I nod and tell her that yes I'm alright. There is such sadness in her eyes. She knows something. She knows about me. I drop my notebook and she picks it up and hands it to me again.

I open the notebook and go through the pages. I've only written a few words: "My name is Ann. It was easy to start killing."

Nothing more, only some notes about making explosives, at the back of the notebook, and something else, about sacrifice. I smile to myself. When did I write that? Such melodrama. It seems like years before. I remember. That first night in Jimmy and Kaz's apartment, when we got drunk and swore revenge on The System. The kind of dramatic, silly thing a schoolgirl would write. So strange.

I look up. The woman smiles, tells me to rest and finally leaves. She thinks I'm crazy. I'm all alone now. Did she say my name? I can't be sure. I'm sad to see that she's really gone.

I feel something on the seat beside me. I'm shocked to see it. I freeze. It's full of meaning to me. A little plastic flower. It must have been the woman who left it. I stare at it a long time before

I pick it up. No, she can't be alive. I try and get up. Maybe she's on the train somewhere. Maybe it was all a mistake. She's here. The flower is her signal. She needs my help. I'll take her with me. She can do whatever she wants. I'll be her life now. Anywhere she wants. I can't make any more decisions. I need her. She's wiser than I am. So much smarter.

I'm not sure if I'm imagining it. My eyes fill with tears. So that was it. It was that clear. There would never be any need to arrest me. No, they're wrong. I would show them. Just some rest. If the woman comes back I'll ask her about my family. I'll ask her to take the flower and give it to my mother to remember me by. I'll try and stay awake until the little girl comes back. Then I'll finally ask about her name.

Maybe one regret. I should have done that prick Vecchio. For Jimmy and Kaz. I should have finally given him that reward he was always talking about. Maybe I could go back and see my mom and little brother. The police would have backed off by then, it would be calmer. In the meantime I'll send them money. I'll try and talk to Jimmy and Kaz's families. I'll tell them how they were heroes. How they tried. I'll tell them where their sons are buried, so they can have some peace about that. I'll at least try and make them understand.

I'm so thirsty. In a little bit I'll ask for some water when the conductor comes around, then rest some more. I remember now, about the woman. She was the teller who spoke with Jimmy inside the bank. The nexus building. She was the one in the restroom, in the train station. The one in the photograph in the line outside the building. She seems to be everywhere.

The woman comes back again. What was I supposed to ask her? I can't remember. She is giving me something to drink. It's not water, it's something else. At first I refuse. It tastes good. I feel a little better. She smiles at me and wipes my brow. I am so cold and wet. She gets a blanket and wraps it around me. She smiles but I can see how sad she is. Am I making her sad?

We'll see. It won't be long until Chicago. I wonder what their tunnels are like. I wonder if there are other creatures down there. Like the man in the suit. Or others like us, like Jimmy and me and Kaz, who still believe. Maybe it's The System that's already breeding them down there. To do what it wants them to.

I'm not sure, but I think I saw the man in the suit pass the compartment and look inside for a moment. He is talking to someone outside the compartment, but I can't see who it is. Another man maybe. I think I can hear my name mentioned again, but I can't be sure. The woman wipes my brow again and tells me to sleep.

When she leaves I'm alone again. I look for my notebook but can't find it. It probably just fell on the floor. There's nobody here to pick it up for me. I'll find it later. After some sleep.

The man in the suit comes in. I think it's the first time that I really look at him closely. I'm not sure if he is there to help me or kill me. He's so small, like a hobbit, like a little toy. He's completely bald. I don't think he weighs more than a child. His eyes are large and bright, like they need to suck in and save as much light as they can. He's so thin. The skin of his face is pulled back away from his teeth, exposing his gums. It's grotesque.

I can't be sure he's real. I reach out and touch him and he smiles, showing his gums again. Is it his suit or some kind of protective skin? It's much cleaner than a few days ago, that time in the tunnels.

No, he's not human. The tunnels have created him. He's come out of the subway. A new race to try and make everything right again. Fight The System. Go ahead, pick a number. I wish him luck.

He picks up something from the floor and puts it in the palm of my hand. It's the little plastic flower. He curls my fingers around it. I won't let it go again. He looks so sad. Why? The battle above ground must not be going great. I ask him what he believes. I never had a chance that time, in the tunnels. I ask him if it's worth it, what he's doing, but he doesn't answer me. There is doubt in those strange grey eyes. No, he's not sure at all. Whatever it is, it's also something about me, I know it is. And he's not sure about it. He's not telling me.

Instead he says goodbye and says he's sorry. Why? Is he the one who shot me? Where is he going? On a trip somewhere.

That's right, we're on a train. Back to the tunnels? Am I going with him and the woman? I panic for a moment. I can't go back there. I tell him I can't go back.

Was he the one who shot me? I have to know.

He tells me that it was one of the policemen. It was done before he could be stopped.

I begin to move, to struggle. I can't go back. The woman enters and helps the man in the suit calm me down. They tell me not to worry, that I won't ever go into the tunnels again. The man in the suit says something to the woman. She leaves again.

When we're alone the man in the suit comes closer. He kneels in front of me and strokes my hair.

I tell him that I did what he wanted. I'm ashamed to say it. Somewhere there is still hope that I can be free, that I can survive, that there is compassion in this man kneeling in front of me, kneeling like he's giving me my last rites.

He tells me that he knows. That he understands. That he would have done the same thing in my place.

"At some point, Ann," he tells me, "we have to trust."

I ignore what he says and instead tell him that we were once thinking of hitting the FBI offices at Federal Plaza. That I regret now that we didn't. He smiles at how silly it all seems. Of course he knows about it. He always knew.

I ask him if I'll see my family again. He says yes, but first I have to sleep, get some rest. I have to be rested to see my family. Then get showered and cleaned up. What would my mother say if she saw me looking like this? He's right. I know I'm a mess.

I ask him if he'll let my mother know about me, about what happened to me, how I died, where I was buried, about Jimmy and Kaz, about everything. Would others know?

He tells me that everyone would know the truth. So that's it. I'm dying, and there's nothing more to be done. There's no chance they'll let me go now, not with what I know. They've secured the compartment. There's only one thing left.

Then he has the nerve to ask me why I didn't go to the warehouse, why I didn't trust him. I can see that it's bothering him.

I tell him that it wouldn't have made any difference.

I know now that he's lying, that he was always lying. I was right in the first place.

I tell him to go fuck himself, the self-complaisant prick. Don't insult me anymore. I've had enough. I tell him to go back to the tunnels.

Before he leaves he tells me one more thing, that he will get Vecchio. Yeah, sure. Enough lies.

He hesitates, as though trying to decide whether or not I believe him. Why does it mean so much to him? I'm silent, I don't say a thing. Then he gets up and leaves and closes the door behind him. It's done. Over. There's nothing more to say.

I'm alone again. Here, in another small space. Maybe for good. I'm glad.

Maybe they'll finally leave me alone, let me go. If I sit still and be quiet, it'll all pass, they'll be gone. I'll be safe.

For a moment I believe I'm back under the city again. But there's something bright hurting my eyes. A light bulb? No, it's light coming through the window. I can see trees and houses whipping by, like a movie. Are we still and is it the outside moving past us? It's making me dizzy. It's so bright, I close my eyes. I'm excited about this trip. Maybe my family is here with me somewhere on the train. I'm so happy. There is a chance, there is hope again. Hope of laughing with my mother again, of playing with my little brother. Get better. Wipe the slate clean and start again. Begin to take it all down, one piece at a time. All or nothing. Such a good feeling, this sense of purpose. Nothing like it.

I start to get mad again.

Fuck them. This is what they wanted all along. This is how it all starts again. And you don't know a thing about it. You just have to put the glasses on again to see what's really in front of you, that it's all worth it. That you need to fuck The System. That it needs to be fucked. It's waiting to be fucked.

I find my notebook sitting in my lap. Did the man in the suit leave it there? I take my notebook and start to write again: *alright, I know it's ridiculous and I never believed we could change anything. But we were excited just talking about it, I can't tell you what a lift it gave us, that sense of purpose in our lives, even though it all sounds like bullshit now. It gave meaning to our lives, like we were finally given an answer to why we were here.*

I have to write it down this time. I don't want to forget that feeling. The feeling I had when we first started.

I remember reading somewhere that one country fought another country so many times, for so long, that their soldiers ended up looking just like each other. You couldn't tell one side from the other. They became each other. Crazy. But I could see it happening everywhere. There was nothing outside it.

I think it's too late for me now. I'm like one of those sleepwalkers who doesn't want to wake up. I just want to keep walking somewhere. I don't want to wake up. As long as I'm walking, marching along. Muscle memory. I have to do it. As soon as I leave this train.

No, I'll have to try something else, something completely illogical. Just once. Maybe I'll live. I'll go on living. How's that for screwing up their logic. That would show them. No, the man in the suit would be ready for it, and waiting. Maybe there was nothing really left to do except die. Maybe on my own terms at least. They could at least give me that much.

I think again of that night we burned the books. The time we made that pact early on not to get trapped by any ideology. We didn't believe in any of them…anarchy, nihilism, socialism, fucking social Darwinists, you name it. I still don't. All bullshit. Somebody always wants to lead and they always want others to follow. That's the way it is. That's the way it'll always be.

I still believe that. I do. Even now. I write that down too so I won't disappear. If I write, I'm still here. I'm still here.

Jimmy was right. It's when you get to that point when you don't care about your life anymore, that's when you can do things, that's when you can have power. That's when your head becomes clear and you see the choices ahead of you. All lit up clearly, like airport runways at night. That's when you know what choice to make. That's where I am now.

All I ever wanted was to be with Jimmy. That's all.

I think Jimmy knew when he looked at me, that last time in the tunnels. I think he knew that I had finally reached that point. Could he see it in my face? In my eyes? That I can follow the lights now. That it can only lead us to each other in the end, no matter which path I take. It always will. There's nothing more to fear. I'm free now. So is Jimmy.

I have to stop writing for a time. I'm too tired. And the pain is coming back a little. I have to write more, but I need to wait a bit, and then I'll write. Only a short pause. That's all. I don't want to disappear.

I'm happy. I don't feel alone anymore, for the first time in days. I don't give a shit if it was right or wrong. The thing is, we thought it was right. That's all that ever matters.

Yeah, I'll come back and fuck all of them. They think they have me. They want me to sleepwalk, just keep moving and buying, moving and buying like all the others. Let my guilt eat me up, keep me in line, keep my head low. Maybe I'll go to confession and say my Hail Marys. Then go shopping. Fuck 'em all. Fuck 'em. I'm not going to make it easy for them. Here I am again running right at the lion, one last time. I'm never going to make it easy for them.

Everything is clear again. The glasses are back in place. I'm glad.

My anger will take care of me. It always does. Hate makes everything clear. I can see again. I know what to do. I know how to move again. There is just one thing in front of me now. One more thing to do. It's all so simple.

Another odd thing. Nobody except Copernik asked me why we did what we did. The only one who seemed interested or cared to know was a corrupt cop. Go figure. Nobody else seemed to give a shit, like none of it mattered, like it was all just another piece of violence lost among so many other pieces of violence. Maybe I'm reading too much into it. It wouldn't be the first time. Maybe everybody was just being polite. Yeah sure.

I just have to wait, just a little longer. That thing that was always with us, always out to destroy us. Fuck it too. I'll take it all down, one little piece at a time.

Out of the blue I think of something and start laughing. It's my mind playing tricks again. It's just that, now that I think about it, all that time down there in the tunnels, I don't think we took the subway once. Never rode in one of the cars once. All that time we were down there. I don't think Jimmy or I ever thought about it. Until now.

I think that's funny.

Epilogue

Police in Rochester report that the body of a young woman was found yesterday evening by an Amtrak employee. The woman was discovered in one of the compartments of Amtrak's lakeshore limited train heading westbound to Chicago from New York. The woman was found after the train had made its scheduled stop in Rochester.

Police say there was no identification on the dead woman, who is thought to be in her late twenties or early thirties.

Although not all details are available – and the authorities have not yet confirmed it – it appears the woman may have been the victim of a gunshot wound.

Police say it could take some time to establish the young woman's identity. Amtrak authorities are cooperating with the Rochester Police and FBI to solve the mystery.

Lightning Source UK Ltd.
Milton Keynes UK
UKOW03f0408080514

231321UK00002B/21/P